"We got off to a pretty bad start, didn't we?" Kate asked.

Tucker smiled. "I imagine you had a life back in the city. Gave it up to come take care of your father. Couldn't have been easy."

Kate lifted her gaze and he saw her eyes deepen. He also saw a fleeting vulnerability along with pain. "My family's everything to me—small as it is. When you shake that down, it wasn't hard to know what I had to do... what I wanted to do. I suppose I didn't think anything else was important."

"Not even a ticket from a small-town sheriff?" he teased gently.

Her laugh was soft. "I'm not going to live that one down, am I?"

"Doubtful."

She looked up at the star-filled sky. "Never realized how inspiring small towns can be."

He looked at the slim column of her neck, the curve of her throat as it arched. Inspiring. It had been a lifetime since he'd stood in the moonlight next to a woman. A lifetime forever unwound.

Books by Bonnie K. Winn

Love Inspired

*A Family All Her Own
*Family Ties
*Promise of Grace
*Protected Hearts
*Child of Mine
*To Love Again
*Lone Star Blessings

*Rosewood, Texas

BONNIE K. WINN

is a hopeless romantic who has written incessantly since the third grade. So it seemed only natural that she turned to romance writing. A seasoned author of historical and contemporary romance, Bonnie has won numerous awards for her bestselling books. *Affaire de Coeur* chose her as one of the Top Ten Romance Writers in America.

Bonnie loves writing contemporary romance because she can set her stories in the modern cities close to her heart and explore the endlessly fascinating strengths of today's women.

Living in the foothills of the Rockies gives her plenty of inspiration and a touch of whimsy, as well. She shares her life with her husband, son and a spunky Norwich terrier who lends his characteristics to many pets in her stories. Bonnie's keeping mum about anyone else's characteristics she may have borrowed.

Lone Star Blessings
Bonnie K. Winn

Steeple
Hill®

Published by Steeple Hill Books™

STEEPLE HILL BOOKS

Steeple Hill®

Recycling programs
for this product may
not exist in your area.

ISBN-13: 978-0-373-81445-9

LONE STAR BLESSINGS

www.SteepleHill.com

Printed in U.S.A.

Why art thou cast down, O my soul?
And why art thou disquieted within me?
Hope in God: for I shall yet praise him who is
the health of my countenance, and my God.
                                    —*Psalms* 43:5

In memory of my parents.
Always loved.
Forever missed.

Deepest thanks to my agent, Danielle Egan-Miller,
for your unwavering support, understanding,
belief, encouragement and friendship.

And, to Melissa Endlich,
for making my return so good.

Chapter One

One mile to Rosewood. Kaitlyn would have done a somersault if she weren't crammed into her small VW Jetta with all her clothes, the entire contents of her bathroom, books, laptop, work supplies and her cat, Noodle, who had been screeching nonstop for the last thirty minutes. Leaving the highway, she pulled on to Main Street. Usually, when she visited her father, she took time to dally down the Victorian, tree-lined avenue. Now, feeling as though she were covered in road film, all she could think of was getting to her father's house, then out of the car.

And she was more tired than she could ever remember being. The exhaustion was both physical and emotional. A few weeks earlier, when Kate had received the news about her father's fall, she'd been concerned, but she hadn't expected anything quite so serious. He'd broken his hip, then as a result, suffered an embolism that could have been fatal. That ruled out staying home on his own. Knowing he didn't want to go to a long-term recovery facility, she'd offered to stay until he could live by himself again. And that would be quite a while. If he had another fall, a second embolism might not be detected until it was too late.

So in the last few days, she'd listed her condo with a Realtor, emptied what mattered into her car, arranged to have the rest moved to storage, and broken her engagement.

She hadn't expected Derek to be wild about her decision to remain with her father until he could live on his own again. But she hadn't anticipated his total lack of understanding. She'd always known his career was terribly important to him, that he had never shown any interest in her family, but... He'd always had an excuse when she invited him to visit her father. And she rationalized his absences to herself. Too much so, she now realized.

She lifted her left hand, now absent her large diamond engagement ring. Derek had been shocked when she returned it. Almost more shocked than hearing she was breaking their engagement.

Kate returned her grip on the steering wheel. Taking pity on Noodle, who was still screeching, she reached over to his crate and unfastened the latch. Poor baby, he hated driving as far as the vet's when they were home in Houston. Three hours on the road had been torture. Smiling, she pulled open the door of his crate.

White fur erupted. Claws extended, Noodle flipped back on to the top of his crate, bolted up on the car seat and landed on Kaitlyn's shoulders. Hair standing on end, he dug in his claws. She swerved over the white stripe in the middle of the road, trying to pull him off. Noodle just dug in deeper. Jerking the wheel in the opposite direction, she tried to reach her terrified pet. A few swerves later, she peeled his paws from her shoulders and he clutched on to the headrest.

She exhaled, then sucked in her breath when a siren suddenly shrilled behind her. Noodle screeched as well, jumping on top of her head.

Kate came to a stop somewhere near the side of the road. It was hard to tell, with Noodle obscuring her vision. Sweaty, exhausted and frustrated, she tried to unfasten his claws, but Noodle was having none of it.

Someone knocked on her window and she jumped, bumping Noodle into the headliner. Seeing it was a policeman, she rolled down the window.

His gaze roamed over her cat and the crammed car, but his critical expression didn't change. "Nice hat."

Closing her eyes, she counted silently to ten. "Don't tell me you pulled me over for a fashion commentary, officer."

"Nope. Left taillight's out. And, it's Sheriff Grey."

Taillight? *Taillight!* She hadn't slept for two days, she was worried sick about her father and now…this…. "I know Rosewood's a sleepy town, but surely you have better things to do than patrol for sinister taillight outages."

"Yeah, we're pretty backward here, but we still don't allow cars to zigzag all over Main Street. You may not have noticed, but people are walking on the sidewalks and the kids are out of school for the day."

She sighed. "I didn't think Noodle would go nuts when I opened his crate. I'm normally a very safe driver."

His Stetson shaded his eyes. "Hmm. License and proof of insurance, please."

Kate couldn't help it. She gaped at him. "I told you—"

"License?"

Muttering under her breath, she dug in her purse and pulled out her driver's license and insurance card from her wallet. Still fuming, she didn't speak as she handed them over.

He gave them a cursory glance. Then he walked back to his patrol car. Well, technically his patrol SUV. She watched him from her side mirror. He was tall, and he slid right into the driver's side without having to step up. She could tell he'd entered her info and was waiting to see if she was a modern-day Ma Barker. As he did, she gently disengaged Noodle's claws and got him back in his crate. She glanced in the rearview mirror, trying to see what the sheriff was doing. Instead, she caught sight of herself.

Egad. Her auburn hair was twisted up on top of her head in a Pebbles ponytail. Wisps had escaped and poked out everywhere. She hadn't bothered with makeup, which meant her light-colored eyebrows and eyelashes were barely visible. Worried about her father, she hadn't paid a bit of attention to her appearance. Her mismatched T-shirt and cotton pants were testament to that fact.

Groaning, she plopped her head back against the seat. *Imagine what that sheriff must be thinking.* Couldn't have been a balding, paunchy middle-aged officer. No, it had to be a hunky guy about her own age. Despite his Stetson, she glimpsed the thick, dark hair that grew just past his neckline. His eyes were equally dark, surprisingly intense. Well over six feet of lean, muscled man.

Still seething, she could see in the mirror that he was writing something. Emerging from the SUV, clipboard in hand, he strolled back to her car.

"I'm citing you for a malfunctioning taillight, Ms. Lambert." He handed her the clipboard. "Sign on the bottom."

Kate gritted her teeth as she signed, then almost jabbed him when she shoved the clipboard back out the window. "Nothing better to do than harass innocent citizens, *Sheriff?*"

"I could have written you up for weaving all over the road—that's a moving violation. This is a fix-it ticket. Send in proof you've had it repaired and the ticket will be dismissed."

Still mad, she accepted the ticket, staring straight ahead. She pushed a button, starting to roll up her window.

"Your license," he reminded her.

She let go of the button, but didn't lower the window, making him reach into the narrow space to return her driver's license and insurance card. When she had them in hand, she finished rolling up the window, then jerked the car in gear.

Although she accelerated as fast as legally possible, she also looked again in the rearview mirror. In all her visits to Rosewood, how had she managed to miss this guy?

Tucker took his time strolling back to the SUV. Once inside he thumped the clipboard back in place. "Nitwit out-of-towners. Wish they'd stay in their cities."

Yet even as he groused about the woman, he wondered who she was, where she was going. That didn't happen often. Tourists who wandered into town from the main highway rarely stayed long when they found out Rosewood wasn't tailored for visitors.

But this one… Looked like she'd filled the car with everything she owned—definitely not the typical visitor. And her unusual green eyes had filled with a fire as unexpected as it was intriguing. He didn't like passing out tickets indiscriminately, but the safety of his citizens trumped a pretty woman any day. Funny, he hadn't thought about a woman's looks since…

He sighed. Not that a day went by that he didn't think of Shelley. But it shocked him that a stranger could make him forget for even a minute.

* * *

After settling Noodle at her father's house, Kate took time to shower and change before driving to the hospital. She glanced at her watch, realizing it had taken longer to bring in her things than she'd planned. That, and unlatching Noodle from the thick living room drapes, where he'd decided to hide.

Kate waved to the nurse at the unit desk, then entered her father's room. "Hey, Dad."

"Hey, yourself. I wasn't expecting you tonight. Thought you'd be unloading your car."

"Done." She put her purse on the bedside table. "Well, a lot of it. I don't have to get everything in tonight. And since the ambulance is bringing you home in the morning, I didn't have to empty my little car."

Marvin shook his silver-haired head. "Who'd have thought one bad step would cause so much bother?"

Kate took his hand. "Hey, none of that. You're my optimist, remember?"

"Here, you're having to take time off...." He sighed.

"Not really. I brought the canvas I'm working on."

"But what about your next project?"

"Clients can find me on my Web site or by

cell." She smiled, determined to lift his spirits. "As long as people have artwork to restore, I can run my business anywhere."

"Still, I promised myself I'd never become a burden."

She blinked away the sting of tears. "You've always carried me, Dad…through everything… especially when Mom died. I'm old enough now to know how hard that was for you, but you never let on." Kate squeezed his hand. "And who wouldn't want a vacation in Rosewood? You picked the perfect place to retire."

That nudged out a smile. "Yeah, it's pretty special. Good-hearted people."

Kate thought of the sheriff, but decided not to pass on that bit of information. "You're ready to be back home."

"Nurses and doctors here are okay, but you know how I feel about hospitals."

Ever since her mother had died, Marvin had a horror of hospitals. It was something she'd strongly factored in when making her decision. He would need months of recuperation. Feeling fiercely protective, she was determined he wouldn't spend it in a long-term recovery facility that would crush his spirit. She knew many of the places were excellent, but that wasn't the issue. He didn't need to mentally return to the worst time in his life.

"When you get home in the morning, you can start recuperating with Noodle."

"Hated the trip?"

"And then some. I expect him to pout for days."

Marvin laughed. It was good to hear. Always an upbeat, charming, strong man, it had been frightening to see him lying in a hospital bed, connected to so many tubes and machines.

They chatted for a little while, and her father understood when she told him she still had to do some grocery shopping. She needed to replenish the fridge and pantry.

Since it had been evening when she arrived at the hospital, Kate had parked near the emergency room, the best nighttime exit. A lot of employees used the same entrance and she could hear the shuffle of their footsteps, the whoosh of automatic doors.

Head down, she dug in her purse for her keys.

"Whoa."

Kate heard the voice, just as two strong hands grasped her arms. She jerked her head up, staring into a broad chest. The man stepped back so she could see his face.

That obstinate sheriff! His height, the boots and hat—no doubt about it.

"Don't you *ever* watch where you're going?" The brim of his Stetson shaded his eyes and she couldn't tell by his voice if he was being sarcastic or teasing.

"This is a hallway, not a racetrack." Abandoning the search for her keys, she echoed his own words from that afternoon. "Lots of pedestrians, you know."

She thought she spotted a glimmer of amusement in his expression.

"You didn't get very far."

Kate drew her eyebrows together, uncomfortably aware that she still hadn't put on any makeup and that she looked a mess. "Excuse me?"

"Aren't you just passing through?"

"What makes you think that?"

"Your car was pretty loaded. Most folks don't spend more than a few days looking at the wildflowers."

"I'm not most folks."

"I sensed that when you let your cat out of his crate. Cats aren't known for enjoying car rides."

So now he was an expert on cats. Kate realized she was grumpy. Tired and worried about her father, she was hard-pressed to be polite. More to the point, she hadn't forgotten the stupid, unnecessary ticket. "Cats *are* allowed in cars here, aren't they?"

It was definitely amusement in his dark eyes. "We don't lock up many drivers for taking their cats along."

Hysterical. "So, what do you lock people up for? Driving down Main Street?"

"Actually, our cells are empty ninety-nine per-cent of the time."

She wasn't amused. It wasn't as though she'd intended to swerve all over the road. And he could have been more understanding about the circumstances. Since he was so tall, she had to tilt her head to meet his eyes, but she did, hoping she conveyed her resentment.

He waited another moment, but when she remained silent, he tipped the brim of his hat. "Got business to see about."

Clutching her purse, she nodded in return.

He walked past her to the ER registration desk.

Don't look! Don't look! And she almost didn't. A foot from the exit, she peeked back. And he wasn't even a mite less impressive.

Tucker Grey pulled into the driveway of his house. His twelve-year-old daughter, Alyssa, had all the lights in the living room on. And as he parked in front of the detached garage that was set back from the house, he could see that she had the kitchen lights on as well. She did that when she was alone. Had ever since her mother died two years ago. He felt guilty that his daughter had to be on her own, but Alyssa now protested she was too old for a babysitter.

He had insisted—until a few months ago, when the only sitter he could find was barely a year older than Alyssa. The lady next door offered, but she was swamped caring for both ailing parents and a new grandchild. Other neighbors had also offered, but Alyssa didn't want to stay at anyone's house—she felt she was always in the way. Still, Rosewood looked after their own; people in town kept an eye out for her, knowing she was a latchkey child and that the Greys didn't have any other family in the area.

Tucker's sister, Karen, had moved away years ago, and she continued campaigning for them to join her family in Iowa. But he was a Texas man, down to the heels of his cowboy boots. Besides, Rosewood was good for his daughter. It was all she'd ever known, and he wasn't about to make her go through any more changes.

Still, it remained difficult for him to open the door and walk into the house, knowing Shelley wasn't there... wouldn't ever be there again. She had made their house a home. Now it was just a place where he slept and ate.

Pushing open the back door, he took off his hat and hung it on a peg. An open bag of potato chips sat on the table along with some sort of dip. He hoped Alyssa had eaten something more substantial for dinner. The television blared in the living room, something else that had begun after Shelley's death.

Stomach down, legs kicking in a crisscross fashion, Alyssa sprawled out on the couch with her homework. He was lucky. She was a good kid, doing what she should without being told. Remembering his own preteen years, he probably would have ditched his homework if his mother hadn't kept at him.

Alyssa looked up, her dark, blunt-cut hair nearly obscuring her eyes. "Hey, Dad."

He picked up the remote and lowered the volume. "Tell me you ate something besides chips."

"Sure." She turned a page in her math book. "I had pizza."

He thought of their stock of frozen food: dinners, microwavable pizzas, egg rolls. It had been a while since they'd had anything else. His hours had lengthened and he rarely got home in time to eat with his daughter. "Sorry I'm late. Accident on the highway."

She sat up, looking at him in genuine concern. "Did anybody get hurt?"

She was so much like her mother. "Not seriously. Mostly scrapes, a broken arm. You have much more homework?"

"I could work on my book report, but it's not due for two weeks, and I want to watch my show."

He smiled. She didn't ask for much. "Sure, Lissy."

She frowned. "Did you eat any dinner?"

Tucker had to think. "I grabbed something around two."

"You have to eat three meals a day," she lectured. "I told you I could make a casserole."

His throat tightened. "You're already doing too much. I don't want you cooking for me as well." Reaching out, he tucked her hair behind one ear. "You're supposed to be a kid. That only comes around once, and I don't want you to miss it."

"Cooking won't make me miss it. I used to help make stuff with Mommy."

Briefly closing his eyes, he tried to keep the pain from his face. "I know. Listen, I'm going to be better about getting home earlier." For some reason, after Shelley's death, he couldn't get as much done in a regular workday. It was as though he carried a hundred-pound stone around his neck, weighing down his thoughts and actions.

"It's okay, Dad." She shrugged. "You can't just leave, like if you worked in a store or something."

No. But Shelley was no longer there to make sure Alyssa was properly being taken care of.

She stacked her books and folders on the coffee table. "I'll make you a sandwich."

"I can do that."

She shook her head. "You'll forget. I'm writing a new shopping list, with stuff that's not frozen. We're supposed to be eating vegetables, you know."

He always made sure they had frozen dinners with vegetables, but he guessed that wouldn't be a convincing argument. "Even peas?"

She made a face. "Vegetables we *like*."

"Ah. Then no broccoli for me."

"Deal." Alyssa headed into the kitchen.

He followed, feeling neglectful and guilty. "Lissy, you want to eat dinner at the café?"

"Not really. I'm kinda full. And my show starts in a few minutes."

"Right." He *had* to do better; his child couldn't raise herself. He just wasn't sure how he was going to pull it off.

Chapter Two

Kate's dad, Marvin, had only been home a few days when he started getting restless. He'd had a stream of visitors—neighbors and members of his church. She had met some of them when they visited at the hospital. In fact, that's how she'd found the contractor, Seth McAllister, who was making the house wheelchair-accessible. He and his wife, Emma, had offered to help. When Kate asked for the name of a good local contractor, Seth had volunteered. Later, another visitor told her how lucky she was to have snagged him, since he usually worked on larger projects.

Emma had helped keep Kate company during some of the many hours she'd spent at the hospital while her father was recuperating. Kate had protested that she was taking too much of Emma's time, but the other woman waved away her objections. It was a Rosewood thing, she'd insisted.

During those hours, Kate learned that Emma had been a newcomer to Rosewood a few years earlier. Formerly an attorney, she'd been relocated to Rosewood while in the witness protection program. Sadly, her husband and daughter had been killed when a criminal attempted to murder Emma by setting fire to her house.

Once in Rosewood, Emma had opened a costume shop and literally fell in love with the man next door. Seth lived on his own, having lost his son to leukemia, his wife to divorce. Although he'd planned to never open his heart again, Emma had crept past his defenses. Together they adopted Toby, a boy who needed them as much as they needed him. Their family had nearly doubled when their twins, Everitt and Logan, were born. Now, the twins were rambunctious two-year-olds.

And Seth was coming over in a little while to take measurements for widening a few more doorways. He'd already rushed to reconfigure the bathroom before Marvin came home.

"Do you want a snack, Dad? Your friends have brought over everything from cupcakes to lasagna." Fresh, homemade bread, cakes, pies and casseroles, even a batch of his favorite—fudge.

"Maybe later, Katie." He petted Noodle. "Just

laying around doesn't work up much of an appetite."

"Seth should be here soon. He suggested we take down most of the wall that separates the living room from the entry, so you can turn your chair easily."

Startled, Marvin jerked his attention from the cat. "What do you think of that?"

"Actually, it'll open up the space. I know it'll take some getting used to, changes always do."

Marvin's eyes darkened.

Kate knew he hadn't yet adjusted to his limitations. "But the room'll still be cozy, especially since it has that gorgeous stone fireplace." She perched on the side of his bed. "I know you're going batty, Dad. Once you can wheel into the living room, you'll be able to see what's going on outside." The living room had a big picture window that looked out on to the street. And the physical therapist had ordered a wheelchair with special leg rests that would allow Marvin to get out of bed. With luck, it should come soon.

"Just think about it, Dad. If you want to keep the living room like it is, we'll move the furniture around and make it work."

The doorbell rang and Kate rose. "That's probably Seth."

Kate was delighted to see that it was Seth and he'd brought Emma and Toby along.

Seth held up a television. "Emma thought Marvin might be getting bored. This set isn't too big, but it has a built-in DVD player."

"He'll love it." She closed the door. "He's pretty antsy."

Emma gave a mock shudder. "Drives me nuts when I'm stuck in bed."

Kate gestured for them to follow her toward Marvin's bedroom.

Emma rested one hand on her son's shoulders. "Toby's a ruthless Monopoly player. Think your dad would like a game?"

"He loves games—*any* kind. Thanks, Toby."

The boy shrugged, embarrassed to be the center of attention. "I don't like being sick, either."

"Hey, Marvin," Seth greeted the older man.

"Seth, good to see you!" Marvin sat up a bit straighter, pleased by the company. "And Emma! You look prettier every time I see you."

She blushed, looking almost too young to be a wife and mother.

"Hey, Toby. Whatcha got there?" Marvin asked.

"Monopoly." Toby held up the Texas edition. "Mom thought you'd like it."

"She's right." Marvin rubbed his hands together in anticipation.

"We left the twins with a sitter," Emma told Kate. "You know they get into everything they see."

"Especially my stuff," Toby added, as he laid out the game on the hospital-style bed table that Kate had rented. "But they're okay." Big brother pride crept through, making them all smile.

Seth placed the television on one end of the dresser. "I'll run a line for cable," he mused. "Won't take a minute. The connection must be close, since the TV in the living room has a satellite converter."

Kate was overwhelmed by the generosity of her father's friends. "You all are great."

Emma waved away the words. "I feel bad that I haven't been over much since Marvin came home. During the week, it's harder to get a sitter—and trust me, Everitt and Logan aren't a good combo with anything that's not totally indestructible."

Marvin looked up from the game pieces. "I'm not fragile, you know."

"Of course not. But the twins are like little tanks. Toby had a science project he'd been working on for weeks. They totaled it in about three minutes. By the time I figured out they'd learned how to get around the baby gate, his project was history."

"That must have been tough," Marvin sympathized.

"They didn't know better," Toby excused them, as he counted out the Monopoly money.

Kate met Emma's proud, touched gaze. "That's quite a boy you have there."

"That's for sure," Emma agreed, her turquoise eyes suspiciously moist. "He's a gift from the Lord."

Emma had confided that Toby had been abandoned by his family and it was the boy's faith in Seth that had broken down her husband's defenses, allowing him to include Toby and Emma in his heart.

Seth pressed his wife's shoulder affectionately, then headed outside.

Emma regained her composure. "I didn't bring over any food, because I figured you'd be deluged with it. Thought I'd wait till next week. Would Saturday be okay? I'd like to bring you something for Sunday dinner."

"That's not necessary," Kate protested.

"Sure isn't," Marvin chimed in. "Next week's the first Sunday of the month, potluck lunch after church services. We can stay, eat there."

Surprised, Kate stared at her father. "You don't think you're going to church that soon?"

He picked the dog for his Monopoly piece and plunked it on the game board. "Don't see why not."

Kate had her hands full with him at home. How could she take him to church? "For starters, you don't have your specialized wheelchair yet."

"The therapist said I'd have it by Monday," Marvin replied. He slanted a glance at Emma. "Say, have you found anyone to teach the girls' Sunday school class? What are they, about ten?"

"Twelve, actually. Preteens. And, no." Emma shook back her blond hair. "Jennifer Laroy was great with them, but now that she's moved, well... It's always hardest to get teachers for the teenagers. Got to have someone with energy."

"Kate's got a ton of energy," Marvin mused. "Do her good to have someone to talk to besides me."

Gaping at her father, Kate tried to fashion a courteous rebuttal.

"Would you really be interested?" Emma's voice bloomed with enthusiasm. "The girls would be thrilled. They're all fascinated with city life, since they've only lived in Rosewood."

"Well, I... I have to be here to take care of my father—"

"Nope. Soon as I have that wheelchair, I'm going to church." His no-nonsense tone of voice was one she remembered from earlier years.

"We'll have to clear it with your doctor..." Kate tried to imagine the logistics of getting him out so soon.

"The church has a van that's equipped with a lift," Emma informed them. "We use it for the school as well."

"The church is only three blocks away," Marvin interrupted. "What do you say, Kate? We can walk that far."

Roll, you mean.

He looked too hopeful to refuse. "I suppose."

Emma clapped her hands together. "Wonderful! I'll send the materials for the lesson over with Seth, so you can have plenty of time to get ready. I'm so pleased!"

She hadn't meant that she agreed to teach. Kate looked at Emma, then at her father. Their faces were beaming. His was the brightest it had been since his fall.

Fait accompli. She hadn't attended church in at least five years, and she'd just signed up to teach Sunday school. *Sunday school!*

Tucker filled a bowl with some of the oatmeal Alyssa had insisted on making for him. Since it was Sunday, he decided he could forego his routine of only black coffee.

These days, he rarely awoke with an appetite. As a kid, he loved Sunday breakfasts. His mother always made something special—French toast or waffles. And Shelley had done much the same.

Alyssa hadn't forgotten about her expanded shopping list. They'd resupplied the pantry and filled the refrigerator. He still didn't want his daughter doing so much, but his workdays hadn't shortened yet.

"Dad?" Alyssa bounced into the kitchen.

"I'm eating the oatmeal."

"Good." She stubbed the toes of her shoes against the wooden floor, first one foot, then the other. "Um...I was wondering if you'd go to church with me."

He pulled his eyebrows together, his forehead wrinkling. "You know I don't go to church anymore." Not since Shelley died.

She fiddled with the top rung on one of the chairs. "But today's special. I'm getting a new Sunday school teacher."

Tucker released the spoon, allowing it to slide into the warm cereal. "Lissy, I want you to be happy, but..." All the unanswered prayers he'd said for Shelley floated before him, reminding him of the bitter result.

She swallowed, her face downcast. "I just thought, you know, how we have a picnic lunch after...and...it's families..."

Tucker's clenched jaw twitched. "You can sit with your friends."

Alyssa shrugged halfheartedly. "Yeah. I guess."

He'd never intended to deny her anything. She was the most important thing in his life. But the betrayal he felt was so deep, still so raw.... Initially, he'd wanted to forbid her from attending church. But he could picture Shelley's disappointed face, and he hadn't been able to take that final, irreversible step. "Come here, Pop-tart."

Her feet dragged as she walked around the table toward him.

He hugged her, wishing it could be different, wishing everything hadn't gone so terribly wrong. "I love you, Lissy."

Hugging back, she sniffled. "Me, too."

"Tell you what. I'll walk with you to church, or drive if you want."

"Walk," she decided, still looking unhappy, tearing at his heart.

He shoved the uneaten oatmeal aside. "How 'bout if I come back when church is out, share the picnic with you?"

Her face transformed in an instant, and she grabbed his neck in a fierce hug. "Thanks, Dad."

His heart constricted as he hugged her back. "Okay, scoot. We have to get ready." Even though he didn't intend to enter the church building, his years of being a member mandated he dress appropriately.

It didn't take him long to change into a suit. Straightening his tie, he stared hard in the mirror, his voice barely audible. *"Just so you know, Lord, this is for Lissy, not me."*

The clatter of Alyssa's shoes on the wood floor made him spin around and walk back into the kitchen. "You ready?"

"Yeah." She grabbed her bible from the counter. "When Grandma called, she said they're going to California on vacation, but she'll call you before they leave." Shelley's parents lived in Dallas, but they kept in touch by phone and regular visits, and the Sunday morning phone call had become a ritual.

"Grandpa got his way, huh?" He smiled as the screen door banged closed behind them. "A fishing trip?"

"Grandma didn't seem to mind." Alyssa hopped down the front steps.

Their neighborhood was one of the oldest in Rosewood, and Main Street was barely six blocks over. Since Rosewood had been settled in the nineteenth century, many of the houses were Victorian. Not being a planned community, small houses often flanked larger, more ornate ones. The oak and elm trees were old, tall and broad, lining the streets and sidewalks. As they walked the few blocks toward church, the scent of late-blooming roses infused the air. Most of the century-old bushes should have been long dormant, but the mild Hill Country weather allowed a long season.

Tucker and Alyssa weren't the only ones walking to church. Most of their neighbors chose to leave their cars home on clear Sundays. They'd covered one block when Alyssa tugged on his sleeve. "Look, Dad."

Some woman was trying to back over the stone curb with a man in a wheelchair. He had only a rear view of them, but he could see they were having trouble. Tucker hastened his gait. "Whoa! Let me give you a hand."

The woman muttered something that he couldn't quite make out. When he reached them, she turned her head. *It was her.*

"I'll ease the chair over the curb, if you'll watch the leg rests," Tucker offered.

"Thank you." Kate gritted the words out through clenched teeth as she tugged on the handles again, making no progress. "It seems stuck."

She was as cordial as he remembered. Having seen her at the hospital, he assumed she must be some sort of health worker—which made sense, seeing her now.

Once the chair cleared the curb, Tucker turned it toward the church. "I'm guessing you're headed this way."

"Thanks." The older man sounded greatly relieved. "I'm Marvin Lambert."

"Tucker Grey." He extended his hand, surprised

by the strong shake from the older man. "And, this is my daughter, Alyssa. I don't think I've met you."

Alyssa waved at them both.

"I retired here about a year and a half ago." Marvin gestured to the chair. "And, I'm not getting out as much these days." He pointed to the woman. "This is my daughter, Kate."

The name clicked and he made the connection. Nodding to her, Tucker grasped the handles of the chair. "I recommend you stay on the street side instead of the sidewalk, sir."

"Marvin."

"Agreed." Tucker ignored Kate's startled expression as he took charge of the wheelchair. "We don't have those updated sidewalks where the curb slopes down at the end of each block. But the street's safe enough. The kids ride their bikes on this one all the time."

Kate looked anxious. "I didn't think about the curbs when we started this adventure."

"At the church you can roll right up the driveway," Alyssa added helpfully, falling into step beside Kate.

"I'm glad to hear it." Kate adjusted her purse strap. "I should have allowed more time to get there. You ought to go on ahead of us, we'll slow you down."

Tucker didn't release the handles. He liked

watching the woman fidget. He could tell by the look of her that she didn't give up control easily. Normally, that was a trait he admired. But she'd been prickly since she'd wheeled into town.

Though his stride was brisk, Kate kept up with him. "Really. I can take over now."

She was as pretty as he remembered, especially with the stubborn set of her chin. "No problem. We're going the same way."

Kate muttered something beneath her breath.

Tucker smiled. The morning was looking up. With Kate on one side, Alyssa next to her, they walked down the street, three abreast. "So, didn't want to try driving again in town?"

Gritting her teeth, Kate glanced at the girl. "It's only a few blocks. Not much point in taking the car."

They passed an older couple strolling slowly down the sidewalk. Tucker bent forward. "Marvin, I bet you like getting out in the air."

"Yep."

Tucker glanced at Kate. She refrained from commenting, but her chin jutted out a fraction farther. So he probed a bit more. "You from the city?"

Pursing her lips, she definitely looked irked. "Any particular one? Texas alone has three of the biggest in the country."

So her temper was still touchy. Matched the

deep blaze of her hair. He couldn't help thinking, if she looked this good angry, she must really be something when she smiled.

Once they arrived at the church, Marvin was surrounded by welcoming members. Many of their faces were familiar to Kate—people who had visited Marvin at the hospital or at home. A man offered to take over the reins, and wheeled Marvin toward the Sunday school building. Her father waved jauntily, clearly happy to be back among friends. As he rolled away, Kate turned to speak with Tucker. Realizing she'd acted grouchy, she intended to thank him for his help...but couldn't see him anywhere. Even his daughter had disappeared.

Feeling ridiculously bereft, Kate wondered where her class was held. She was usually pretty organized, but she hadn't thought to ask Emma. The Community Church was a good-size set of buildings. The lovely old chapel stretched upward toward equally aged trees, the sunlight reflecting off the tall, multicolored stained glass panes. She guessed the second structure was the Sunday school building, plenty large enough for her to wander in for a while without finding her class.

"Kate!"

Recognizing Emma's voice, she turned to see

the entire McAllister clan, including the infamous twins, who were as adorable as she'd imagined.

"I just realized I didn't tell you where your classroom is," Emma began. "We have a short general meeting in the gym before we break into individual classes." She turned to her husband. "Honey, can you take Logan and Everitt to the nursery so I can show Kate around?"

"Sure." Seth glanced at their older son. "As long as I get Toby to help."

As the guys left, Kate grinned at the image of this strapping man having difficulty wrangling two-year-olds.

"Thanks for steering me in the right direction, Emma. I haven't told you—but it's, um…been a while since I've been to church. One more reason I'm nervous about teaching this class."

"The Lord will be with you." Emma's expression was encouraging. "Trust me, there won't be any awkward silences. Twelve-year-old girls never run out of things to talk about."

"Good." Kate clasped the teacher's edition of the Sunday school lesson book. "I studied the materials, and at one time I was a regular at Sunday school, but I've never been a teacher."

"That's okay. Just be yourself and the girls will love you."

"The last time I had anything to do with pre-teens, I was twelve myself."

Emma laughed. "You *are* a good sport. Your dad and I kind of bulldozed you into teaching."

"Agreed," she replied with a wry smile, "but seeing Dad so happy…well, I'm grateful you and the other members are such good friends to him."

"Marvin's great. I've always thought he ought to have a passel of grandkids."

Kate grimaced, remembering the abrupt end of her engagement. "Afraid that's not going to happen. At least not in the foreseeable future."

"I didn't mean to pry—"

"You didn't." Kate cleared her throat, remembering how Emma had confided in her, trusting her, treating her as a friend, not an acquaintance. "My fiancé couldn't cope with me coming here to help out Dad. So…"

Emma linked her elbow with Kate's. "I'm sorry. Maybe he'll come around."

Kate shook her head. "Family's not important to him—something I was way too late noticing. And it is to me—important, I mean."

"Marvin's always talked about you," Emma confided. "He's so proud of you."

"You know I don't have any siblings, so Dad and I have always been close…I don't want that to ever change."

"In my book, you made the right decision. And, honestly, I try not to put my nose in anyone's business, but maybe Marvin's break was a lucky one for you. It's not always easy to learn what a person's all about before you marry."

"But you and Seth…"

Emma grinned. "I'm the luckiest woman on the planet. Our marriage gets better every day. Just when I think it couldn't possibly improve even a fraction, it does."

"Like I've said before, you guys are a living Norman Rockwell portrait."

"I believe you're a true romantic, Kate Lambert. I keep hearing we're a dying breed."

"Probably for good reason. Talk about embarrassing, I planned to marry the man and never even thought to ask about family."

Emma squeezed her arm. "When we love someone, we excuse a lot of things we wouldn't otherwise."

"How'd you get to be so wise?"

A shadow flickered in Emma's eyes. "Not wise, observant."

"Oh, Emma!" Kate was stricken. "I'm so sorry. I didn't mean to bring up—"

"It's okay. Really. They're always in my heart, too. I've been so blessed. Not everyone gets a second chance…a second family."

Incredibly grateful that Emma was her first friend in Rosewood, Kate stayed by her side as they arrived at the general assembly. The opening prayer, announcements and one hymn passed too quickly.

Emma walked with her to the girls' classroom, then gave her a discreet thumbs up. Even more nervous, Kate gingerly stepped inside and took a chair. She watched the girls enter, bidding them hello. They all looked curious. Rosewood was a small town—one where almost everyone knew each other. And she stuck out like the proverbial sore thumb.

Some of her uneasiness disappeared as she recognized the sheriff's daughter. When all the chairs were filled, Kate addressed the small group. "Hi. My name's Kate Lambert. I'm going to be in Rosewood for a while, taking care of my father. And I'll be teaching your class for however long that is."

The girls stared at her. Silence.

"Um, why don't you tell me something about yourselves?" Kate smiled at the curious faces. "Let's start with Alyssa."

Each of the girls gave her a few basic facts. They were all in the same grade and had known each other since nursery school days.

"Miss Laroy let us have a slumber party at her house," Sasha announced.

"And we had our own booth at Harvest Festival," Amber chimed in.

"Well…" Kate took a deep breath, hoping she looked composed. "Why don't we wait a bit to discuss activities?" She held up her Sunday school book. "Did everyone read this week's lesson?"

Various answers tumbled out.

Kate regained most of her footing as the lesson progressed. She wouldn't compare Sunday school to riding a bike, but everything was coming back to her. Still, she was relieved when the first bell rang, indicating time to finish up. Since Alyssa had remained interested and upbeat, Kate asked her to say the closing prayer.

Bending her head, she listened to the girl's words. They were about what she expected until almost the end.

"…and bless the ones we love and please make them love You."

They all chimed in when Alyssa said amen. Opening her eyes, Kate studied the girl, watching as Alyssa unclenched her hands. And wondered what was troubling her so.

Chapter Three

Tucker leaned against the broad trunk of a live oak tree on the north lawn of the church, the heel of one boot braced on the rough bark. He'd had to dust his dress boots, since he hadn't worn them in a while. It seemed strange to stand in front of the church, a place he'd practically grown up in. When he was a kid, unless blood or loss of limb was imminent, his family was in church every week. His mother used to say that if she missed church, the whole week was off because it didn't have a beginning.

When he was eighteen, his parents were killed in a car wreck. The pastor had helped Tucker and his older sister through the loss. Karen had married and moved out of state not long afterwards. Although losing his parents had torn him up, Tucker had reconciled the loss by knowing that his parents were together forever, that neither would have been happy without the other.

Then he met Shelley and was certain that his theory was right. They were married in the chapel, and when Alyssa came along, they'd had her blessed in the same spot. And now it was the one place he couldn't bear to enter.

As he watched, the tall, wide sanctuary doors pushed open, and people spilled out onto the front steps. Strands of conversation and laughter floated in the air like early spring butterflies. He could make out snatches of words; others were muffled by the footsteps of children who rushed out, anxious to be in the fresh air, ready to begin the picnic.

The first Sunday of the month potluck had been a tradition since he was a boy. On the rare occasions when bad weather clouded the skies, and during the winter months, they met in the Sunday school building. But his mother always said the Lord smiled on Sundays, that's why it was usually sunny.

Alyssa sprinted toward him, her face one huge smile. "You came!"

Tucker's gut clenched. Had he been that neglectful? He draped a hand over her shoulders. "Couldn't keep me away." His full attention on his daughter, he didn't notice the approach of several surprised, pleased-looking members.

"Tuck, I thought it was you!" Grinning, Michael Carlson pumped his hand, then clapped the other on Tucker's shoulder. "It's been too long."

Before Tucker could respond, several of the other people zoomed in, all talking at once. He must have shaken two dozen hands within mere minutes.

"So glad to see you!" Emma McAllister hugged him, then drew back with a big smile.

"We've missed you," Matt Whitaker added.

Assorted versions of the same sentiment echoed as people crowded around. Although Tucker had known many of them since he was a kid, he didn't feel a sense of homecoming. Instead, he felt the distance he'd created since Shelley's death. He managed to say most of the right words, respond to all the greetings. However, the tie he was no longer accustomed to wearing seemed to tighten.

He glanced at Alyssa, and her expression was one of pure pleasure. Knowing he couldn't disappoint her, he allowed himself to be swept along as the members strolled toward the back lawn, where round tables and folding chairs had been set up. Some people opted to bring quilts and sit on the lawn, but Tucker had been so caught up in the trauma of coming to the church, he hadn't thought to bring a blanket or a dish to share. Long, rectangular tables, draped with plain white table-cloths, were filled with casseroles, salads, cakes, fried chicken—just about everything.

Families clustered together. Tucker swallowed, remembering when he was a kid and his parents would bring a quilt, so they could sit beneath the spreading limbs of the tallest oak tree.

Alyssa tugged on his hand. "Miss Emma said it's okay we didn't bring anything, 'cause there's always too much anyway."

True. He'd never yet been to a potluck that ran short of food. He wasn't particularly hungry, wishing only that the picnic would end quickly so he could go home. But he walked behind Alyssa, scooping food onto his paper plate, then filling a glass of punch.

"This way, Dad." Alyssa scooted toward a table.

Trying to balance the plate and glass, he didn't notice until it was too late that she'd led him to the Lambert woman's table.

"Miss Lambert's my new Sunday school teacher," Alyssa announced, clearly pleased.

That was quick. She'd barely had time to unpack her car.

Marvin greeted him heartily. "Come sit down."

He couldn't refuse without being rude. "Sure we won't be crowding you?"

Marvin shook his head, gesturing to his wheelchair. "I brought my own seating, so we have more than enough room. Right, Kate?"

She met Tucker's gaze and he was surprised to see a trace of vulnerability in her eyes. It faded quickly as she directed her attention toward Alyssa. "Hey!"

Alyssa scooted into the narrow spot between Marvin and Kate. There wasn't a chair on the other side of Marvin, but there was one beside Kate. Moving the chair would be awkward, obvious. So he put his plate on the table and sat next to her.

His shoulder brushed hers as he settled in place. She didn't jerk away, but he could feel her arm stiffen before he shifted over a few inches.

Sipping his punch, he wished he'd thought to choose a bracing cup of coffee instead. He watched his daughter. Her face was lit up, more animated than he'd seen it in…longer than he could calculate.

Marvin cut into his brisket. "Did you get some of this, Tucker? Best brisket I've ever eaten. That's saying something—I eat barbecue at least twice a week."

Tucker hadn't paid any particular attention to what he'd piled on his plate. Looking at it, he realized he had about three kinds of potato salad and no meat. "I'll have to try it another time."

"I can get you some, Dad." Alyssa popped up before he could protest.

Marvin looked after her wistfully. "Wish I could bottle some of that energy."

Tucker guessed Marvin was a man used to doing things on his own. He was probably chafing, being confined to that chair.

"Does she have any brothers or sisters?" Kate asked.

His throat tightened. "No."

She didn't press. "I'm an only child myself."

Marvin looked over at Tucker, then wrinkled his brow. "How is it I've never met you? I've been coming to this church since I moved here."

Alyssa arrived with a hearty portion of brisket. "Mr. Carlson said there's lots." After placing the plate of meat on the table, she scooted next to Kate again. "And there's all kinds of cake, too."

Marvin turned his attention to the girl. "Daisy Ford didn't make a pie?"

Alyssa shrugged. "Somebody said there weren't many pies 'cause there's gonna be a pie sale for the hospital this week. Guess they want to make sure people'll buy the pies."

Marvin nodded. "That's right. Just heard about it this morning. My brain's starting to act like a sieve."

"It's okay to forget stuff," Alyssa assured him. "I forget things, too."

Marvin chuckled. "Guess I'll take your word for it."

Tucker watched them, remembering the light, easy play they'd shared with Alyssa's grandparents. But now the visits were one-sided. Shelley's parents drove down from Dallas, but he and Alyssa hadn't been out of Rosewood in the last two years.

Kate picked up the plate of brisket, offering it to him. "It really is delicious. Somebody told me that Michael Carlson cooks it over a low fire for hours and hours. I'm not that much of a meat eater, but this just melts in your mouth."

His gaze dropped to her lips as she spoke. They seemed to be curved in a perpetual smile. Well, at least since they'd sat down to lunch. He easily remembered how well she could frown. Still, he couldn't miss the tint of some sort of pinkish gloss on her full lips.

At that thought, he straightened up so quickly that he brushed her arm again. His tie felt as though it was made of shrinking elastic, tightening around his neck. "Warm for this time of year, isn't it?"

Kate tilted her head. "I've only visited here before, so I don't really know, but it seems about right to me."

"She's used to the heat and humidity in Houston,"

Marvin explained. "It's like being in a twenty-four hour sauna."

Tucker glanced back at Kate. "So you *are* from the city."

"Born and bred."

He waited, but she didn't add any details. Picking at the food on his plate, he hoped they wouldn't have to stay too long at the lunch. He glanced over at his daughter. Alyssa was all smiles.

And she'd sure taken to Kate.

Something was different about the woman, but he couldn't put his finger on the change. Same fiery green eyes, pale skin, auburn hair…maybe that was it—she didn't have her hair scrunched into a ponytail. Instead it was loose, falling past her shoulders in waves.

Pretending interest in his brisket, he snuck another look. With her coloring, he expected a sprinkling of freckles, but he didn't see any. Maybe she was a hothouse flower who kept inside all the time. She laughed just then at something Alyssa said, throwing back her head, exposing the slim column of her throat. It, too, appeared flawless.

"Tucker, it's been a month of Sundays!" Old man Carruthers stopped by the table. "Well, more than that, I think. Good to see you back where you belong."

Tucker stood to shake his hand. Albert Carruthers had been Tucker's Sunday school teacher when he was in junior high school. Despite his feelings about church now, Tucker knew Mr. Carruthers only meant well.

"You doing all right, sir?"

"Just getting old, Tuck." He lifted his cane. "But I'm not letting it slow me down."

Remembering the older man's endless energy when he was younger, Tucker grinned and lightly touched the cane. "Don't be vaulting any fences. Mrs. Carruthers'll have your hide."

Albert chuckled. "You're right about that." Reaching up, he patted Tucker's shoulder. "Don't be a stranger. I've missed you."

Tucker would have liked to reassure his old friend, but he couldn't lie to him.

When Mr. Carruthers left to stroll toward his wife, Tucker sat down.

Kate looked at him curiously. "Sounds like you're the prodigal son."

He clenched his jaw, aware of his daughter's close proximity. "Do you think you've been in town long enough to judge that?"

Kate had the kind of face that didn't hide what she was thinking. And he saw curiosity turn to puzzled concern. "I just noticed a lot of people surprised to…" She glanced at Alyssa and apparently had a flash of good sense. "This is all new to me. Nice, but new." Picking up a cup of punch, she averted her face.

Tucker felt the brush of her shoulder as she fidgeted. She put down the plastic cup, fiddled with her fork, then straightened out her paper napkin. "So, anyone ready for dessert?"

Marvin and Alyssa looked down at their nearly full plates.

Tucker studied Kate.

Apparently, he wasn't the only one who wanted to bolt.

That afternoon, Marvin whistled as he sat in front of the large window in the living room. Since Seth had removed the barrier to the entry, he could maneuver easily without help. As he watched the day dwindle toward its end, couples strolled down the street, some hand in hand. Young parents pushed strollers and children shrieked as they let off the last remnants of energy.

Kate brought him a glass of iced tea. "I'll have to remember to buy some more lemons."

"This is one of my favorite things on Sunday." He pointed out the window. "Reminds me of when I was a kid...when it wasn't so frantic in Houston. It just got too big too fast."

"Pace is slower here," she agreed. "I keep forgetting I don't have to rush somewhere every day and plan, so that I can avoid traffic and lines."

"I had enough of both." Marvin shook his head. "Didn't like feeling I was always running, never catching up. Pace here suits me better."

"Are you hungry? It's getting close to dinner time."

Marvin shrugged. "A little, maybe. That was a big lunch."

Kate watched as an older couple strolled by. "Looks like they've been together forever."

"The Hills? About fifty years."

"Incredible. That's what? Two-thirds of their lives?"

"Sounds about right. Katie, you haven't even mentioned Derek."

She'd dreaded this conversation. "There's nothing to talk about."

"Has he called since you've been here?"

"We've got lasagna and baked ham left. You choose. When all the good stuff's gone, you'll be stuck with my cooking, which you know is terrible. That or sandwiches." She fluffed the pillows on the couch. "Then again, maybe I'll just get take-out from the café so I don't poison you."

"Did you argue about coming here to take care of me?"

She sighed. "He wasn't who I thought he was."

"I assume that's a figurative reference."

"Maybe I didn't *want* to see the real Derek."

"This is because of me. Katie, I won't let you ruin your life—"

"Dad, coming here just opened my eyes. And I'm glad. What if I'd stumbled into marriage, then found out? It hurts, but it's better to know."

He sighed. "Confession—ever since I moved here, I've hoped that someday you would, too. Now I've trapped you."

"You can't trap somebody who volunteers. Face it, you couldn't have kept me away."

"So much like your mother. Stubborn, kind, seeing the best in people."

There were days when Kate missed her mother so badly it was as though she'd just barely died, instead of twenty-five years ago. Blinking away the tears, she looked at the floor. "So, lasagna or ham?"

"She'd be proud of you, Katie."

"We can make sandwiches out of the ham, so let's have lasagna. I do know how to warm up stuff in the microwave. But no promises about not burning it. I usually make TV dinners because they have the instructions right on the package."

"Katie?"

"Yes, Dad?"

"Love you."

"Yeah. Me, too."

Chapter Four

Kate reached high with the feather duster, passing it over the top of the bureau in her father's room. A second later she heard knocking. She glanced down at her jeans and mussed shirt. Fortunately, none of their visitors seemed to notice her perpetual state of messiness. Still, she smoothed her hair back as she reached the front door and opened it.

Alyssa Grey stood on the porch, looking somewhat shy.

"Hey! What a pleasant surprise. Come in."

The girl looked at the duster still in Kate's hand. "Are you busy?"

Realizing she'd forgotten to ditch the duster, Kate stuck it behind her back. "You are a very welcome diversion. I don't mind housework, but I like company better."

"Is your dad okay, Miss Lambert?"

"Kate. And yes, he's fine." She noticed Alyssa had her backpack on. "Did you just get out of school?"

"Uh-huh. I passed your house on the way home, so…"

Kate sensed the girl was feeling uncertain. "I'm glad you have time to stop and visit. How about a snack?" She headed into the kitchen, Alyssa trailing behind. "We've got some fruit, um… cheese…yogurt…"

"I'm okay."

Reaching into the fruit drawer, Kate pulled out two apples. "Want one?"

"Sure."

They settled at the kitchen table, companionably munching their apples. "So you don't live far?"

Alyssa pointed north. "About a block that way."

"Great, we're neighbors!" She reached for a paper napkin. "Did you let your parents know that you were stopping here?"

She shook her head. "It's just my dad, and he's at work."

"Oh." Kate cleared her throat. She had wondered on Sunday where the girl's mother was. "Shouldn't you still check in?"

"In a few minutes. Dad got me a cell phone

after... Anyway, I'm not supposed to use it to talk to friends, just if I need him. So I call from home. But we got out an hour early—it's Teacher Day or something."

Kate wasn't thrilled that this likeable girl belonged to the obstinate sheriff, but she knew how parents worried. "Surely he knows that."

"He's got a hard job and he forgets little stuff."

Like when his daughter was due home? He shot down further in her estimation. Sure, divorce was difficult, but if he had primary custody, he needed to step it up. Not something she wanted to say to this child. "Okay, you have to be completely honest with me. Did I stink at teaching your class?"

Alyssa giggled. "Everybody likes you. Sasha's worried you won't let us have as many parties as Miss Laroy, but it's cool that you lived in Houston and you're an artist."

"I restore paintings—so I'm a fixer, not an artist." She leaned forward. "I haven't taught a Sunday school class in a really long time. Think everyone will give me time to get my footing?"

"Sure. Miss Laroy moved away."

Kate laughed aloud. The frankness of youth.

"I thought I heard somebody." Marvin rolled into the room, then scrunched his brows in concentration. "Alyssa?"

The girl beamed, pleased that he remembered her name. "Uh-huh. How do you feel?"

"Still rolling."

She giggled.

And Marvin grinned in return.

Kate could see that a dose of Alyssa would be very good for her father. "We're having a snack. You hungry?"

He shook his head. "I'm still stuffed from lunch. Mrs. Ford makes a killer lasagna, but I overdid."

"It's about gone." Kate sighed. "Then you're in for my cooking, and it won't be pretty."

"I can cook," Alyssa offered, shy again.

"That makes one of us." Kate glanced at the nearly bare counters. "I wouldn't mind if the neighbors started bringing over goodies again. We had almost every kind of cake and pie, and—"

"That reminds me," Marvin interrupted, "I volunteered you to make a pie for the hospital bake sale tomorrow."

"A *pie?*" She stared at her father in disbelief. "You know I can't cook."

"Making a pie's not cooking. It's just fruit and crust."

Kate rolled her eyes. "You think so? Um, a little detail. I haven't the faintest idea how to make crust. For that matter, I don't know what goes in the filling."

"I do." Alyssa's voice was quiet, but her face looked hopeful.

"Really?" This child was a wonder.

"Some people buy canned filling, but it's easy with real fruit—and it tastes better. We have some peaches that'd make a good pie."

"I can't let you do that!"

"Why not?" Alyssa's large dark eyes grew rounder in expectation.

"Well...I imagine you want to see your friends...and it's an imposition."

"I have to go home and call my dad anyway. I could get the peaches and come back."

Kate stared helplessly at her father.

True to form, he was a big help. "Sounds good to me. Kate teaches you Sunday school, you teach her how to make a pie."

Alyssa grinned, then hopped up. "I'll be right back."

After she scooted out the back door, Kate pinned her father in a chiding gaze. "What was that?"

"You can see the child's hungry for attention." Marvin's grin faded. "Reminds me of another little girl a long time ago."

"Oh, Dad." Reaching out, she patted his hand. "You're such a softie. I thought I noticed something on Sunday, too. Hmm. Her parents are divorced, but I imagine her mother's still part of her life." Kate pursed her lips. "You get all the gossip. What do you know?"

He shrugged. "I didn't meet her father until you did. Seems I heard something about him…. Can't remember just what it was."

Kate sighed. "Do you know if you have a pie pan?"

Marvin shrugged.

"Great. This may be a square pie." She stood and began rummaging in the cabinets. "At least you have flour and sugar." She sniffed the bag of flour, not sure how to tell if it was stale. "Do you know what goes in crust?"

Marvin shrugged. "Nope."

"Would you do me a favor?"

"Anything, Katie."

"Don't volunteer me for anything else."

He chuckled. "Small towns aren't like the city. Everybody gets involved."

"I think I have enough involvement to last for some time."

Nearly an hour later, a light knock sounded on the back door.

Kate opened it. Seeing that Alyssa's hands were full, Kate reached out to help unload them.

"I'm sorry I took so long, but I thought you might not have a pie pan or some of the other stuff we'll need."

"Good guess."

"I need to make a second trip. I'll be right back."

She popped out the door again and Marvin laughed. "She's got enough energy for half a dozen people."

"Youth, Dad."

"Speaking from your own advanced years?" he retorted.

"I never thought about it much before. But I look around and see other women my age with two or three kids, and…"

"When the time's right and the man's right, you'll know."

"You sound very sure."

"Experience, kiddo. I hit the jackpot with your mother."

Her throat tightened as she thought of Derek. She'd chosen so very poorly. How could she know that she'd ever get it right?

"We start on the crust first," Alyssa told her, once she'd brought over all the ingredients. "'Cause it needs to be cold."

Kate frowned. "But if we make it first, won't it get warm?"

"We put the dough in the fridge and let it chill while we make the filling."

Marvin chuckled.

Alyssa put a rolling pin on the counter. "Do you have butter?"

Now wary, Kate thought for a second. "How much do we need?"

"A stick. But it has to be real cold."

Kate exhaled. "No problem."

Marvin turned his chair toward the living room. "You ladies enjoy yourselves."

"Deserter," Kate mumbled under her breath, searching through the cabinets for the bowls.

Once everything was assembled, Alyssa patiently showed Kate the steps in making the crust. It took some time, but eventually the dough was patted into a ball, wrapped in plastic and stowed in the refrigerator. Kate was wearing nearly as much flour as they'd used in the crust, but she was impressed with their results. "I didn't know this could actually be fun."

Alyssa stared at the peach she was peeling, not meeting Kate's eyes. "How come you don't know how to cook?"

She dredged up a smile. "I never learned. When I was seven, my mom died. Dad knew how to grill most everything, so basically, except for cereal and sandwiches, we ate barbecue every day. On the upside, I've never wanted fried food."

Alyssa was suddenly quiet.

Kate knew that death was a difficult concept for children. "Cooking always looks so complicated, on TV shows, I mean."

"You're doing really good." Alyssa handed her a peach. "It's not important how much you know, but how hard you try."

What a mature thought for a young girl.

"I brought the spices," Alyssa continued. "They're not real fresh, so we'll have to use extra."

"Hmm." Kate picked up the bottle of cinnamon, studying the label. "How do you know?"

"Spices last about six months, the ones that are all ground up don't last as long as whole ones. And they put dates on the bottom."

Kate felt about as smart as she had in algebra class. All the other kids got it right away. Not her. "You know a lot for a person your age."

Alyssa shrugged skinny shoulders.

"So, what you said about the importance of trying hard? Did you just come up with that now?"

She shook her head. "It's what my dad says."

Maybe he was a better father than she'd imagined. Once all the fruit was sliced, the sugar and spices added, Kate felt like they'd run a marathon. She glanced at the clock. "Alyssa, was it all right with your dad to stay so long?"

"I left a message at his office."

Feeling a flash of uneasiness, Kate paused. "Then you didn't ask?"

"It's no big deal. I leave messages all the time. He has to work really long days."

"All the time?"

Alyssa was instantly defensive. "The sheriff can't just go home when he wants to. He does important stuff."

"Of course he does." Kate recognized the fierce protectiveness. She remembered feeling the same way about her own father. "I'm happy for your company. Works out for both of us."

A smile edged back on Alyssa's face. "Now you can learn how to put the crust in the pan."

"Oh." Algebra time again.

It took forever to roll out the dough. Alyssa was patient when Kate got dough stuck to the rolling pin and tore it repeatedly.

"Are you sure this is going to be edible?"

Alyssa laughed. At nearly the same moment, the bell at the front door rang steadily, as though someone was leaning on it. Then an equally loud knocking followed.

Marvin hollered through the noise. "Come in!"

Kate reached for a towel, hearing another man's voice in the living room. Before she could finish wiping her hands, she heard the man stomping through the house toward the kitchen.

Tucker's scowl was ferocious. He looked around the kitchen, taking in the domestic scene.

Not wanting the child to get in trouble, Kate stepped toward him, resisting the urge to hide Alyssa behind her. "I'm sorry if we've taken too much of your daughter's time. You know, she's in my Sunday school class. Um... I'm new to it, just started, that is." She linked her fingers together, trying not to visibly clench her hands. "Anyway, I have to bake a pie and I didn't know how, so Alyssa rescued me, volunteering to help. Well, actually to make it...."

"Do you know how I've spent the last hour?" His voice was a near growl, low but controlled. "Calling all of Alyssa's friends, knocking on almost every door in the neighborhood, checking the school, calling on my deputies and nearly everyone I know to search the rest of town."

More intimidated than she wanted to admit, Kate gulped. "She couldn't reach you at the office, so she left a message."

"And you think that's acceptable?"

Kate opened her mouth but couldn't find the right words without implicating Alyssa. "In hindsight, I suppose not. Trust me, if I'd known it would cause trouble…well, I would have done things differently."

"Trust you? I don't even know you." He turned to Alyssa. "Why didn't you answer your cell phone?"

"I'm sorry, Dad. I left it in my backpack." She scrunched her thin shoulders inward. "I didn't think I needed it."

"We've gone over this. When you're away from the house, you carry your cell."

She ducked her head. "I got all excited about the pie…."

Exasperated, his tone lightened a fraction. "How do you even know how to make a pie?"

"Mommy taught me."

Tucker's face paled.

Seeing the swift shaft of pain filling his dark eyes, Kate put her arm around Alyssa's shoulder. "You've raised a wonderful child. My father and I have thoroughly enjoyed her company. In fact, Dad hasn't smiled this much since before the accident."

"Oh." He hesitated. "I don't want Alyssa to be a bother."

Tightening her grip, Kate gave Alyssa a small hug. "She's anything but a bother. She's an absolute joy." Releasing her, Kate grabbed the notepad and pen by the phone. She scribbled their phone number and handed the scrap of paper to him. "She's welcome here any time."

Stiffly, he accepted the number.

"Can I stay, Dad? Kate doesn't know how to do the crust, and if she doesn't do the top part right it could explode."

Tucker didn't speak for several moments. When he did, his voice was grudging. "Just until the pie's done. Then call me so I can walk you home."

It was only a block, but neither Kate nor Alyssa wanted to argue the point.

Tucker left via the back door. It was quiet until Alyssa spoke. "He doesn't mean to sound all mad. He just worries lots more now."

"Now?"

"Since Mommy died."

Kate felt a surprising sting of tears she refused to shed in front of Alyssa. "No wonder he worries so much about you. My dad always has, too."

A wisdom far outweighing her years settled in the girl's eyes. "He misses her a lot."

Kate smoothed the jagged hair on Alyssa's forehead. "You, too."

"Uh-huh." The shadows in her eyes deepened.

There were no words Kate could offer, no glib assurances, no comfort. The pain of losing a mother couldn't be soothed or talked away. Kate felt her heart break a bit, wishing she could absorb Alyssa's pain. Having lived the same loss, she wished even more that she could spare this child.

Alyssa looked upward, her sweet face troubled. "I didn't mean to make you feel bad."

Another piece of her heart crumbled. "You've made me feel better than I have in a long, long time." Kneeling down, Kate hugged her again, vowing to make sure this latchkey child wasn't lonely any longer.

Chapter Five

Tucker shoved his hat back on his head and sighed. "Ralph, I don't imagine Wilbur built the fence over too far on purpose."

Ralph scowled. "He knows how valuable Hill Country land's getting. So he's poaching some of mine."

"It's exactly where the old fence was!" Wilbur shot back.

The men had been arguing for what seemed like hours. Ralph's wife, Cloris, had phoned Tucker, telling him he'd better come over before they tore each other's heads off. Tucker didn't think they'd come to blows, but he wished they'd settle down.

He squinted in the bright noonday sun. It was hot for September. And it occurred to him that Alyssa was right—he ought to eat regular meals.

He'd skipped breakfast and lunch and his stomach was growling, but the men's loud voices drowned out the sound.

"Ralph," Tucker interrupted. "If you didn't have a problem with the old fence, why are you so mad about the new one?"

"Like I said, this land's worth more every day. That old fence was wrong—five feet over the line, but it'd been there more than fifty years."

"My survey says it's on my side," Wilbur insisted, waggling his finger in his neighbor's face.

"What survey?" Ralph demanded.

"The one my pa had done."

Ralph snorted. "That must have been eighty years ago at least!"

"So what? The land hasn't moved. It's not like there's a river running between us."

Patience gone, Tucker sharpened his tone. "Wilbur, you plan on selling your spread?"

"Of course not!"

"Ralph?"

"No, but—"

"If, and only if, one of you decides to sell, then you'll have to get an up-to-date survey. Until then, nothing's changed since the old fence came down and the new one was put up. I want you to quit arguing. Ralph, Cloris is waiting lunch on you. And Wilbur, don't put up any more new fencing until you get a survey." Tucker repositioned his hat, shading his eyes. "Agreed?"

Both men muttered incomprehensibly. Since they'd stopped yelling, Tucker decided to call it done.

He walked toward the SUV. As he did, their voices rose again, the fight renewed.

"Unless you want me to haul you to town for disturbing the peace, you'll both stop right now," Tucker warned.

Wilbur and Ralph stared at him. Neither of them had ever heard Tucker utter a threat, even a mild one.

In the silence, Tucker slid inside the patrol car. Once the engine was running, he flipped the air-conditioning to high. Glancing up, he saw the men still staring.

Not too long ago, he'd have stayed with them until they hammered out a genuine agreement. It wasn't easy, playing peacemaker when he felt like a wound-up coil. He'd been the sheriff in Rosewood for years, deputy before that. But he'd never followed a rigid set of rules. Instead, he dealt with matters as they came up. Now each encounter took longer, eroding his patience.

Frustrated, he headed back toward town. He'd been born in Rosewood, growing up in the gently rolling hills. He knew the name of every wild-flower that populated the fields each spring, the twists and turns of the river, even when they could expect the trees to blaze in autumn. But he didn't know how to find his way back to the kind of life he'd once had.

Kate looked out the living room window, watching for Alyssa. She hadn't stopped by since Tucker had found her in the Lambert kitchen.

"A watched clock won't move," Marvin told her as he rolled into the room.

"I think you have that mixed up with a watched pot. I don't particularly want the clock to boil." She leaned forward, trying to see farther down the sidewalk, tapping her fingers on the sill.

"The sheriff doesn't seem like a bad guy."

"He didn't hesitate biting *my* head off," she reminded him.

"Because he thought something had happened to his daughter. Perfectly reasonable, to my way of thinking."

"Then why hasn't Alyssa been over?"

He shook his head. "Being a parent isn't all that simple."

"I don't recall saying it was."

"Kate, a single father worries every hour of every day about his daughter."

She left the window. "Would you like a cup of tea?"

"I usually have coffee." But they both knew she made terrible coffee.

"There's not much to mess up making tea. Just drop the bag into hot water," she coaxed. "Mrs. Ford brought over that chicken and rice thing you like so much. We won't starve just yet."

"Nice woman. Makes the best pie I've ever had."

Kate thought of the widow who was about her father's age. Her daily visits helped break up Marvin's long days. "So, tea?"

"I'll pass."

"Suit yourself." Kate returned to the window, spotting Alyssa. "She's almost to our house." She bolted from the window, then rushed to yank open the door.

"Any faster and you'll take off for outer space," Marvin observed.

Kate was already down the front steps, heading for the sidewalk. Anxious, she waited as Alyssa slowly reached her. "Hi! How are you?"

Alyssa stubbed the toe of her tennies at a crack in the sidewalk. "Okay."

Kate didn't think she was okay. "I hope I didn't get you into too much trouble."

"Nah." Reluctantly Alyssa lifted her head, meeting Kate's eyes. "I'm grounded."

"Oh no!"

"It's for a week. I don't have that much longer."

"I'm sorry." Kate patted the girl's arm. "I should have realized how worried your father would be."

Alyssa scrunched her skinny shoulders. Clad in her usual T-shirt and denim overalls, she could easily have been mistaken for a boy. Kate had the urge to buy her dresses, barrettes and nail polish. Instead, she smiled. "Mrs. Ford brought a new casserole over today."

That edged out a smile. "You still burning stuff?"

"We're lucky I haven't blown up the kitchen."

The statement reminded them both of making the pie and their smiles faded.

"Would you like me to talk to your dad?" Kate offered, feeling terrible that the child was being punished for something Kate should have controlled better.

"Nah."

Kate bit down on her lip to stop herself from saying anything more.

"I better get home," Alyssa continued. "I have to call my dad and let him know I got there okay."

Kate rubbed her folded arms. "Sure."

Alyssa had taken only a few steps toward her house when Kate called out. "I hope you'll come by again when you're not grounded. I mean, if it's okay with your dad."

A shy smile erased the woebegone look on Alyssa's face. "I'll ask!" Her footsteps lightened as she darted down the sidewalk.

Turning back to the still open front door, Kate pictured the girl home by herself until the sheriff finally made it home. She'd wait until Alyssa's punishment was over. But if that man didn't allow her to come over, Kate intended to get involved. Lagging, she retraced her steps up the sidewalk and porch steps.

Marvin looked at her in concern. "You're moving a whole lot slower than when you catapulted out there."

"She's grounded."

"Sounds reasonable."

Kate jerked her head up to meet his gaze. "I thought you liked Alyssa."

"That's not the point. A lot of youngsters get in trouble because they never had rules, or anyone to enforce them."

"Still, it seems like a harsh punishment."

"Katie, you can't interfere in the way a man chooses to parent his child. I'm guessing she's not grounded forever."

Absentmindedly, Kate wrapped one finger around a bit of hair and wound it in a corkscrew motion. "I can't help thinking she's special. Not just because she's a whiz in the kitchen. She seems so much older than her years, and I'm not convinced that's a good thing."

"Do you remember making Sunday dinner about a month after your mother died?" His smile was wry when Kate shook her head. "You decided nothing would do but fried chicken and the works. You even made bread. The meat was burned on the outside, still raw on the inside. The bread barely rose and came out tasting like bagels. Those little dough Frisbees turned out to be the only edible thing on the table. You know why you were upset? Because you couldn't cook as well as your mother. Without saying a word, you'd decided you had to grow up all at once."

Swallowing, Kate remembered that feeling. Worse, she'd thought she'd failed her father. She *had* grown up pretty quickly. But it seemed so much starker with Alyssa. At least Marvin had been home every day, just over an hour after school let out. And, until she was in junior high, she'd had to spend that short time each afternoon with the lady next door. But Alyssa came home every day to an empty house, never knowing when her father would arrive. "Do you think it's a bad idea for Alyssa to come over here in the afternoons?"

"Depends on what her father says."

"I'd try to ingratiate him by bringing him some sort of dish, but the way I cook…." Kate sighed. "He'd think I was trying to poison him." She glanced past her father to the ceramic casserole dish that held their evening meal.

Sensing her thoughts, Marvin preempted any such notion. "Daisy cooked that for us, and I'm not giving it away."

"Daisy?" Kate smirked, then quickly lifted her hand to cover it. "Anything I need to know?"

"Plenty. But it doesn't happen to be about Daisy Ford. There's a cookbook in one of the kitchen drawers."

"Just because I can read doesn't mean I can cook." Kate had spent her time from college to the present subsisting on fast food and TV dinners. Probably because she knew nothing would ever live up to the warm coziness of her mother's kitchen. When her mother had baked cinnamon rolls, Kate could smell them from the street, and would come flying into the kitchen to taste the first one. All these years later, Kate could be swamped with a sense of loss when she caught even the barest whiff of cinnamon.

"I suppose we could give them half of the chicken dish," Marvin conceded.

She ruffled his thick silver hair. "You were right. I need to have some patience, and to wait it out until Alyssa's not grounded." He didn't have to remind her that patience had never been her strong suit. But helping Alyssa was worth the wait.

Sunday morning, Kate and Marvin were two of the first members to arrive at church. During general assembly, Kate searched the gym, looking for Alyssa. Disappointed not to see her, she fidgeted until they were dismissed. She couldn't believe the sheriff included Sunday school in Alyssa's grounding. Kate had been grounded more than a time or two herself, and it had never included church.

Fuming under her breath, she hurried to the classroom, intending to arrange the chairs in a circle, making it cozier than a podium and rigid rows. The door was propped open and one chair was already occupied.

"Alyssa!" Surprised and pleased, she grinned. "I was afraid you might not be here today."

"My grounding's not done till Tuesday. Well, tomorrow night, but might as well be Tuesday."

"Ah." Kate plunked her purse in one of the folding chairs. "Has it been pretty rough?"

"I missed the pizza party." Alyssa scrunched her shoulders.

Kate remembered the youth group activity from the sheet Emma had given her. Because of her father's situation, Kate was going to ease into attending the youth department's activities when possible. Luckily, there were plenty of youth teachers to chaperone. Squinting, she tried to recall what else the sheet had listed. "Isn't there another one soon?"

"Yeah." Alyssa glanced down, looking shy. "We watched a new DVD instead, one my Dad got for me."

Taken aback, Kate frowned. "When I got grounded, it was no TV at all."

Alyssa's smile brightened. "Dad doesn't do that. You know he has to work late lots of times, and he doesn't want me to get scared or anything. I have to go straight to school and back, and…"

Kate was instantly anxious. "And?"

"I guess that's about it."

Having imagined an utterly grim week for the child, Kate was stumped. Aside from missing the pizza party, it didn't seem to be much of a punishment at all. "Well, I missed you. So did my dad. Have you asked about coming over again?"

Alyssa stared at her shoes, ones that Kate realized didn't go with her woefully plain dress. "I thought I better wait till tomorrow."

"Good idea." A sudden clatter announced other girls approaching, and Kate lowered her voice. "I'll keep my fingers crossed."

Marvin wheeled into the kitchen, feeling restless. Kate was out front, weeding the flower garden— had been most of the afternoon. Since he loved gardening, he itched to get out there, to work in the manicured beds. He didn't want Kate to know, but he wondered if he ever would.

A light tap sounded on the back door, then it opened. Daisy Ford smiled, looking tentative. "I saw Kate out front. She told me to come on in."

"Well sure." He motioned from the chair, seeing the indecision fade from her pretty blue eyes.

She walked to the counter, putting down the casserole she held. "I thought lasagna might be a change from all the chicken."

Marvin chuckled. He had confided that when Kate was stumped for dinner, she bought fried chicken from the café. Apparently she still thought it was the perfect dish for him. "Did I tell you about when she was seven and tried to cook fried chicken?"

"No, tell me."

As he related the story, he rolled toward the coffeemaker. It was dicey, ensuring that he didn't knock his protruding leg into the cabinets, appliances or the table and chairs. Daisy had brought him a mug tree that she'd placed near the edge of the counter so he could reach the mugs. And she'd moved the coffeemaker forward as well.

He took a fresh mug, carefully poured coffee in it for Daisy, then gave it to her. Although he'd barely known her before the accident, she seemed able to sense what he needed. Rather than treating him like a cripple, she acted as though he was perfectly fine. "Thank you, Marvin. Just what I need." He hadn't noticed when she arrived, but she looked tired.

He poured coffee into his own mug. "Bad night?"

She nodded, picking up his cup and carrying it over to the table with hers. "Made the mistake of watching a scary movie. I know every creak my old house makes, but last night they managed to sound menacing. Silly, I know."

"Nope." He handed her the cream. "When it storms, and branches whack the windows, it always sounds worse than it is, so I know what you mean."

Daisy smiled. "You're being kind."

"Humph."

Surprised, she looked at him, in question.

"You're tired, but you made us lasagna—that makes *you* the kind one."

Her smile widened. "Okay, so we're both nice." She laughed, a soft, light sound.

"Too bad you're tired, I was looking forward to Scrabble."

"Did I say I was too tired for Scrabble?" She wriggled her eyebrows. "You're two games ahead. I can't let you keep that lead."

Daisy was a breath of fresh air. No tiptoeing around, as though he were fragile.

"Okay, one cup of coffee, then we play."

She sipped her coffee. "Two. And I get to go first."

Chuckling, he forgot his restlessness altogether.

Chapter Six

Tucker was exhausted, but he picked at the dinner Alyssa had prepared.

"Don't you like it, Dad?"

"It's great, honey." He reached for a biscuit. "I didn't know you were such a good cook."

"I was afraid the roast might be overdone," she fussed.

"It's perfect." All of it was. She'd fixed mashed potatoes and gravy. And they'd started with a salad. "I'm just tired."

Usually, that would have elicited a lecture on proper nutrition. Instead, Alyssa fiddled with her fork.

"You okay, Lissy?" He hoped she wasn't coming down with something.

Nodding, she lifted one shoulder in a half shrug. "Yeah. Sure."

She didn't sound sure.

Tucker carefully cut a piece of his roast. "What happened at school today?"

"Regular stuff."

"Nothing up with your friends?" He studied her, wishing he could understand what was bothering her. She spent far too much of her energy nurturing him.

"Nope." Reaching for her glass, she took a small sip of tea, then put it back on the table. Only seconds later, she traced a restless finger through the condensation beading on the glass's surface. "Um… Dad?"

Worry clutched at him. "What is it, Lissy?"

"I was wondering…well, you know how I'm not grounded tomorrow? I was wondering if I could go over to Kate's…I mean the Lamberts'." She licked her lips and rushed the last few words. "After school, I mean."

He'd been envisioning a far more serious scenario, but he wasn't pleased. The Lambert woman might teach Sunday school, but she didn't seem very warm and cuddly to him. And he didn't want Alyssa to get hurt—welcome until the woman tired of her, then… Tucker's faith in people wasn't much better than that in God. It had sunk after his wife's death, and had been deteriorating ever since. "Lissy…"

Her eyes were pleading.

"She might be too busy, honey."

Alyssa leaned forward, her expression animated. "No! She invited me. Twice. So, can I?"

A thousand thoughts streaked through his mind. Reluctantly, he put his fork down, picked up his napkin and wiped his lips. "If I say yes—"

She rose in her chair.

"If," he repeated, "I say you can go, I want you to be prepared. Adults sometimes make offers…" He swallowed. "Even promises. But they don't always mean them."

"*You* keep your promises." Loving trust beamed from her eyes.

Emotion crowded his throat. Clearing it, he placed his hand over hers. "That'll never change. But I don't want you to get hurt."

Alyssa curled her fingers under his. "It's okay, Dad. You'll see."

Firming his jaw, he swallowed. He was going to make sure it was.

Kate adjusted the easel so that the morning sunlight hit the painting she was restoring at its best advantage. Now that her dad was settled, she'd set up her work in one corner of the living room. She didn't want to make the room messy, but her dad had insisted she use the spot with the best light. And she enjoyed the sense of tranquility she felt when glancing out on to the quiet, tree-lined street. No roar of traffic, no boom boxes. She'd had a studio in her condo, but it had never felt quite the same. Here, she was grounded in a way that she hadn't been in Houston. It was more than the height of her eighth-floor condo. Here, she could reach out and touch the leaves, the dappled shadows from the sun. More importantly, her feelings were grounded, more in touch with what was real.

She was getting more done—fewer distractions and interruptions. Daisy Ford came over every day, which kept Marvin both busy and happy. They played Scrabble, talked for hours, and often she rolled him around the neighborhood or down to Main Street. Like now. And the quiet was a balm.

The doorbell rang—extra-loud in the near empty house. She glanced at her watch—just ten o'clock. She had to think it. So up popped an interruption.

Still holding a sparse sable brush and cloth, she opened the door.

And tried not to simultaneously drop her jaw.

Tucker Grey stood on the porch. "Miss Lambert."

"Kate," she automatically corrected him.

"I need to speak to you."

She stepped back, giving him enough room to enter. Still shocked to see him, it took a moment to gather her thoughts, then gesture to the living room. "Come in."

The space was open, since the entry hall wall had been removed, and he followed as she crossed the room. She placed her brush on the easel tray, then turned back to him. At a loss for words, she waited for him to speak. As she did, she noticed he'd removed his hat. Sunlight glinted on his dark hair. Up close he seemed even taller, even more masculine. Her eyes flickered over the determined set of his strong jaw, the unsmiling lines of his handsome face.

"I'm here about Alyssa."

"Ah." She pointed to the wing chairs, sitting in one herself.

He seemed reluctant, then sat. "She's got some idea in her head about coming over to your house after school."

Since she enjoyed Alyssa and wanted to help fill the empty hole in the girl's life, Kate knew she had to control her tone. She'd been flip with the sheriff since day one. Taking a deep breath, she lifted her gaze to his. "That's because I invited her."

"Thing is..." He clenched his jaw and she could see a muscle flicker. He had a face that could have landed him in the movies if he'd had the notion. "Alyssa takes what you say literally."

Truly puzzled, she tilted her head, pulling her eyebrows together. "And, that's a problem?"

"I don't want her getting hurt." The blunt words matched the fierce protectiveness in his eyes.

"Of course you don't." Absently, Kate fiddled with the paint-splattered cloth she still held. "I don't understand why you think that would happen."

"Because people get tired of watching someone else's kid. And when that happens, she'll be devastated. Even though you've only known her a few weeks, she thinks you're her friend."

"I am." She paused, knowing friendship didn't happen in an instant. "Well, I want to be. I *intend* to be. I've never met anyone like her." Except maybe herself as a child. "Do you realize how special she is?"

He tightened his grip on the brim of his hat. "She *is* my daughter."

Kate sighed. What she was trying to convey was so complicated that she doubted she could verbalize it. The specialness she spoke of was different than the feeling most parents experienced. She wanted to tell him that Alyssa was wise beyond her years, that in fact, she was missing her childhood. Instead, she looked out the large window as she spoke. "Rosewood's a great place to raise a child. I know I haven't been here all that long, but it's something I sensed right away. And the more people I meet, the more convinced I am."

"Nice observation. But you must have things you need to do, things that don't include a twelve-year-old. The man in your life won't appreciate the distraction."

"The only man in my life is my father."

He raised his eyebrows, and she cautioned herself to be patient. "I broke up with my fiancé, Derek, before I moved here." Wanting to end that subject, she pointed to the painting on her easel. "I'm an art restorer. I can do my work at noon or midnight—set my own schedule. Creates havoc with my insurer, but I can work *where* I want, *when* I want."

For the first time since he'd arrived, he looked—really looked—at the painting. "For museums?"

Surprised he recognized the quality of the piece, she nodded. "After art school, I apprenticed with a big firm. But I like deciding what I work on."

"Being in control?" The challenge in his voice was unmistakable.

"You could call it that."

"What do you call it?"

The challenge intensified. "I like doing things my own way. And I don't apologize for it."

"And when a little girl gets in the way of that?"

Sucker punched, she deflated in an instant. "Alyssa's a child, not a thing! How dare you presume I'd treat her any other way?"

His voice was calm, quiet, controlled. "Because she's *my* child. Alyssa's had to deal with too much pain already. I won't let anyone hurt her—no matter how good their intentions are."

Anger met calm and she fought for control. "So you judge everyone? Or just strangers?"

"It's not a matter of judgment."

"Funny." Her lips trembled with indignation. "That's what you just did. You've barely met me, judged me, found me incompetent."

"Alyssa's not like every other twelve-year-old. She lost her mother, then had to prop me up. I don't take chances where she's concerned."

"Chances?" Anger vibrated deep in her throat.

"Look...Miss—"

"I told you, my name is Kate." Steel slid through her veins, giving her the strength she needed. "Actually, it's Kaitlyn. Kaitlyn Rose Lambert. Rose was my mother's name. My mother who died when I was seven. And, no, I don't have children of my own. But I do know *exactly* how it feels when your mother's gone and the whole world turns gray and nothing makes sense. So, tell me again how lightly I'll take Alyssa's faith in me."

His eyes softened a fraction. Not submissively, but in understanding. "I didn't know."

"You didn't bother to try to find out. I'm not a Rosewood native, so I must be some fly-by-night moron who would hurt a lovely little girl like Alyssa." The harsh words out, Kate clapped one hand over her mouth, hoping she hadn't antagonized him to the point of keeping Alyssa away. "Sorry. I actually do have more than two speeds—besides nice and rabid."

He met her eyes, holding her gaze steadily. His eyes were dark, she realized, but gold flecks made them seem deep, endless. When he broke contact, she guessed he'd made his assessment.

"All right, she can come over. But when you get tired of her hanging around, tell me. And I'll handle it."

As though she would tire of the child… He was not only obstinate, he was the most pessimistic person she'd met. "I'm guessing you're not the glass-is-half-full kind of guy."

He didn't reply.

Wanting to end his visit, she stood. "I have to decide on the color to use, and I can't waste the light."

He stood as well, taking his cue and walking to the door. His hand on the knob, he pulled open the door, then looked back. "Burnt umber."

She drew her eyebrows together.

"The color you need. Burnt umber."

She turned to glance at her painting and he disappeared through the doorway. Frowning, she headed straight to the easel and looked at the spot she was preparing. Burnt umber. He was right. She twisted the cloth in her hands. And wondered if she'd made a premature judgment of her own.

Chapter Seven

Kate dug her spade into the rich, dark soil. She'd been weeding for a few days in the front garden, but today she was overturning the soil, in lieu of using a rototiller. She wanted the beds to be in perfect condition when her father was able to garden again. Refusing to accept that he might not be able to resume what he loved, she stabbed the spade even deeper into the dirt.

"Hey." Alyssa's face appeared tentative.

Delighted to see her, Kate grinned. "I'm so glad it's you."

"Really?" Her shy, pleased smile emerged.

"Absolutely!" Kate rose, brushing off her knees. Seeing Alyssa wore her backpack, she realized the child must have come straight from school. "Daisy and my dad finished playing Scrabble a little while ago—it's getting to be an every day event."

"Your dad's pretty cool."

"I agree. It's been only the two of us forever."

"Just like my dad and me."

Kate couldn't bring herself to agree. "So, grounding's over?"

"Uh-huh. And I asked permission to come over."

Relieved, Kate placed her hand on the child's shoulder. "Do you have much homework?"

"Some."

"After you call your dad and let him know you're here, we can break out the books."

They skirted the front door, heading around the side to the back entry. Kate slipped out of her garden clogs and opened the door. "The phone's on the sideboard."

Alyssa went straight to the phone and punched in a number. "Hi, Dad. I'm at Ka... Miss Lambert's. Uh-huh. Uh-huh. Do you want me to ask? Okay. Bye, Dad."

Kate was itching with curiosity. But she tried to contain it. "How 'bout some fruit punch?"

"Okay." Alyssa put her backpack on the table. "I didn't know grownups liked fruit punch."

"I guessed you might, and I remembered how much I like cherry, so..." She reached for the glass pitcher on an open shelf above the counter, then fished in the pantry for the drink mix. "I'm ready for something cool. I know it's the end of September, but it feels more like August." Once she was at the sink, she tore open the package, then added water. "Would you like to stir while I get some ice?"

"Sure." Alyssa found a long, wooden spoon and carefully mixed the punch.

Kate plunked the ice-filled glasses on the counter, remembering how she'd always been hungry after school. "Want to split a sandwich?"

"Okay. Want me to make it?"

Grinning, Kate reached for the bread. "*This* I can handle. Do you like ham?"

"Uh-huh." She carried their glasses to the kitchen table.

Since her specialty was sandwiches, Kate had stocked up on fragrant bread from the bakery and lunch meat from the local deli.

After a few bites, Alyssa put her sandwich down, then fiddled with her glass. "Dad wanted to know if you were sure it was okay for me to be over here today."

"Very sure." Kate abandoned her own sandwich and patted Alyssa's hand. "He's just worried about you. My dad said he'd always felt that way about me, too. I'm not a parent, but I think I understand. It has to be rough, being the only parent, especially fathers with daughters."

"So it's really okay?"

"Alyssa, I was so bored I was digging in dirt. What do you think?"

The girl's laugh was spontaneous, warm and without reserve.

Within a few minutes they had matching fruit punch mustaches. Alyssa giggled at Kate's.

"Careful, or I'll outline yours in magic marker," Kate teased.

"Did you always like school?" Alyssa asked, her eyes filled with curiosity.

"Most of it. Hated math, though." Kate remembered the joy in transforming her love of painting into real art. "Thank goodness they didn't make me declare a major in junior high. I would have picked makeup and boys."

Alyssa tucked her lower lip behind her front teeth. "Really?"

"I wasn't wild, or anything like that. But I looked at the girls in the teen magazines and thought they were so pretty. And I had the worst crush on Chip Rider. He wasn't even the cutest guy in class, but..." Glancing up, Kate met Alyssa's interested gaze.

"I don't know about makeup, but..." The girl tugged on her hair, then stared for a moment at the table. "Do you think it's dumb to like a guy who doesn't like you?"

Kate felt a rush of memories, warmth, and the immense desire to protect this sweet girl. "If it is, then I'd guess ninety-nine percent of us are dumb. Besides, how do you know…what's his name?"

"Donny Kimball."

"How do you know Donny doesn't like you?"

Alyssa shrugged.

"Maybe he's afraid you don't like him."

Startled, Alyssa's mouth dropped open a fraction.

"Does he go to any of the youth activities?"

"Sometimes. School's having autumn carnival pretty soon, and most everybody goes."

Kate's mind whirled. Alyssa would need something new to wear, a more flattering haircut… Her thoughts screeched to a halt. What would Tucker think of the changes? Looking at Alyssa's hopeful face, Kate squashed the concern. She wasn't planning to turn her into a mini pop star. Just a girl. A little lip gloss, a pretty outfit and a much needed new hair style. Maybe some pale nail polish to match the gloss. "Do you have any half days coming up? Ones where you get out of school early?"

"On Thursday. It's teacher prep day."

Kate smiled as her thoughts spun. She'd talk to Tucker and make sure it was all right for Alyssa to go with her on a few errands. And to make sure he said yes, she'd be positively charming. Even if it killed her.

Tucker shuffled through what seemed a mile-high stack of papers. While paperwork had never been the favorite part of his job, he'd always kept it under control. His chief deputy, Owen Gibson, had eyed the growing pile. But it wasn't Owen's to do. He had his own paperwork to complete.

Theirs was a small office, just two old wooden desks, a few file cabinets and two cells that hadn't been changed in over a century. They rarely had anyone occupy a cell—an occasional driver on the highway who was intoxicated. On the opposite wall, a corkboard held bulletins and photos— luckily, no high-profile criminals sought out their little haven.

Although Rosewood was a quiet town with virtually no crime, he was called by the highway patrol when something happened out on the main thoroughfare. Plus, he had two part-time deputies who patrolled the highway to reduce speeding and accidents. Rosewood had its share of minor infractions and traffic problems—mostly from tourists passing through. But these days, everything had to be documented for the county, state and feds.

Rosewood had resisted the lure of becoming a tourist trap like some Hill Country towns had. No T-shirt or souvenir shops; only one locally owned bed and breakfast. All of the nineteenth-century buildings on Main Street housed thriving businesses—largely due to the fact that the mayor and town council consistently blocked the invasion of any superstores. It might seem like a step back in time to some, but to Tucker it was perfect. When Shelley was alive, they'd spent time roaming the stores, eating ice cream at the marble fountain in the drugstore, meeting up with friends.

The tall stack of papers started sliding. Before he could catch them, they spilled over the side of his desk, cascading in every direction. He heard the door open, but didn't look up. Grabbing a handful of reports, he caught a whiff of soft vanilla, mixed with something he couldn't identify.

Kate dropped her purse on the floor, then bent down on her knees, picking up papers.

Not expecting her, he paused, staring.

"I do this all the time with my paperwork," she began. "Inevitably, it's when I'm working on more than one project and the papers get mixed up. Takes forever to get it all sorted."

"Documentation for the pieces?"

She nodded, continuing to make small stacks.

He sat back on the heels of his boots. "Ever found one that was bogus?"

She crossed her fingers and held them up. "Not yet. Luckily, that's not my job, just the restoration." Her smile was tentative. "I can help sort these, if you'd like."

"Um." He continued collecting reports.

"No wonder you work long hours."

He snapped his head up, his eyes narrowing. "What does that mean?"

She blinked, then cleared her throat. "I just meant, with all this…" She waved at the paper mess. "And your other duties, it must take a lot of time."

He didn't comment, instead shoving everything into one haphazard stack. "I don't imagine you came by to help with my reports."

"Oh." She sat back on her heels.

Tucker stood and offered her a hand. She accepted the gesture and he felt her small, delicate hand for a moment. Silky. The thought popped up, unbidden. He stepped back, using the excuse of dumping his work on the desk.

She pushed her hands in the pockets of her jeans, looking skittish. "I think Alyssa likes coming over after school…to our house, I mean." She flushed. "My father's house. Sorry, my mouth doesn't seem to be connected to my brain. Anyway, I'm thinking of doing a few errands this week and next, and I wondered if you'd mind me taking Alyssa along."

Kate looked different somehow, softer maybe. "Won't she be in the way?"

"Not at all. I'd appreciate the company, actually. I don't know many people in Rosewood except Emma, but she's got her hands full with the twins, so I usually go places alone."

She didn't seem like the sort of person who would mind tackling anything by herself. "I imagine it'd be all right if she doesn't have homework."

Kate pulled her hands from her pockets, apparently needing them to talk. "Or after her homework's done?"

Give her an inch…

"Are you always this pushy? Or is it just with me?"

Her eyes widened, but she recovered quickly. "The time she spends with me keeps her from being alone. Is there some reason you don't want that for her?"

She was like one of those battery commercial bunnies—never giving up. "All right. She can go with you. Just make sure she takes her cell phone."

Kate picked up her purse. "Okay. Have a good day, Tucker."

He watched as she walked stiffly to the door, eased it open, then disappeared.

Sinking into his worn chair, he passed one hand across his forehead. Alyssa meant everything to him, and he wasn't giving her what she deserved. He hated that she'd turned to a stranger. A stranger who, he just realized, had called him Tucker instead of "sheriff" for the first time.

Marvin put the portable phone back in its charger. His last test results had just come in. Virtually no change. At this rate, he'd be a hundred before he healed.

Kate turned on the vacuum cleaner in the living room. Relieved that he didn't have to discuss the doctor's report with her, he wheeled into the kitchen, smelling something heavenly. Couldn't be anything Kate had made.

Daisy stood by the window, the morning sunlight glinting on her pale blond hair. Apparently hearing him, she turned and immediately smiled.

"I knocked, but no one heard me," she began. "So, I let myself in."

"You don't need to knock, Daisy. You know I always want to see you."

Her smile widened. "You're good for me, Marvin Lambert."

"I expect you're welcome wherever you go."

"Pish posh. I had an urge to bake this morning— sticky buns."

"You must have been up at dawn!" He wheeled closer, spotting the luscious-looking platter.

"I always get up early. Did it for so long I couldn't shake the habit after Homer died."

"Yeah. Me, too. And there was Katie, of course."

"You're lucky," she mused, sadness flickering in her eyes.

"We never talked about your children."

"There aren't any. We just weren't blessed that way."

"I'm sorry."

She shrugged. "I'm okay about it most of the time. Then something—usually something little— will remind me what I've missed, and…"

"Is it hard to be around other people's kids?"

"Oh, no! I enjoy children. Most of my friends have grandchildren now, and while maybe I envy them some, I'm glad for them, too." Looking suddenly busy, she turned to the rolls. "These'll taste best warm. 'Course you can heat 'em up in the microwave, too."

"Sacrilege!" he retorted. "Homemade, old-fashioned sticky buns in the microwave? Nope. Besides, what makes you think there'll be any left over?"

That brought the smile back to her face. "You haven't tasted them yet."

"You haven't cooked or baked a clunker yet." He sniffed away. "Umm. Can't get over how they smell."

"If you'll grab the coffee, I'll get some plates, then fetch Kate."

"She wants to get her housework done early. She and Alyssa are up to something this afternoon." Marvin wheeled over to the counter, then picked out two mugs. Kate had made a large pot of coffee already, and left it on the warmer. She was getting better at making coffee—thanks to Daisy's tutelage.

"If I didn't know better, I'd think you were trying to get me alone," Daisy joked.

"Don't think I'm not." He laughed as her jaw froze. "Just you, me and those sticky buns."

Her laughter lifted his spirits. At the same time, he felt a current of truth in the words. Daisy was more than just company. She was…well, she was *Daisy*.

Chapter Eight

At Kate's urging, Alyssa thumbed through the dress rack at Mueller's. Emma had confirmed it was the best store to find clothes for a preteen girl.

Kate held up a yellow outfit, studying it critically. "What are your favorite colors?"

"I'm not sure exactly. When I was little, I liked pink and purple best. I still sorta like 'em, but…"

"You don't want a little-girl pink outfit for the autumn harvest celebration."

"Yeah," she admitted, then ducked her head. "It's cool, how you understand."

"I was once a little girl myself," Kate confided. "Back when the dinosaurs roamed."

Alyssa giggled. "You can't be very old."

"Why's that?"

"'Cause you're not married yet."

Ah, the simple logic of childhood. She didn't

want to shatter that illusion, so she just smiled. "I saw some cute skirts a few rows over."

Alyssa frowned. "I don't have enough of my allowance saved for a dress *and* a skirt."

Kate pulled her into a half hug. "This is *my* treat."

"But—"

"No buts. You don't want to deprive me of doing something I really enjoy?"

"Well, no...but—"

Kate spotted a dress nearly the same color as Alyssa's eyes—a deep blue that reminded her of the ocean near sundown. She took it from the rack and held the dress up.

Alyssa gingerly touched the soft fabric. "It's really pretty."

"Let's set it aside then."

The proprietor, Melba Mueller, didn't hover. But seeing that Kate held onto the dress, offered to put it in a dressing room. They found two skirts, slacks, three tops and a sweater to try on as well.

Kate sat outside the dressing room in a chair put in place for just that purpose. When Alyssa shyly emerged in the blue dress, Kate caught her breath. The girl was a beauty. Beneath the ill-suited haircut and tomboy clothes, a lovely young woman was emerging. "How do you like it, Ally?"

The girl nodded her head in confirmation. "It's great."

Kate grinned. "It suits you. Put it on the peg to the right, okay?"

It didn't take long for Alyssa to change into a skirt and top. She fingered the cute skirt. "This'll add up to too much."

"Tell you what. Let's just hang everything on the right, unless you don't like it. Then we can see what we have." Kate intended to buy her more than one outfit, but she didn't want to overwhelm Alyssa.

Everything she tried on looked perfect. While Alyssa was changing, Kate told Mrs. Mueller her plan. The owner happily agreed to calculate the total and wrap it up while they went to the shoe store. Then Kate could come back, pay for the purchases and pick them up in the morning. Too many packages and Tucker might burst an artery.

Kate then suggested they go to the shoe store to look. It was easy enough to get Alyssa to try on a few pairs. Mentally, Kate chose two pairs Alyssa had lingered over—one casual for school, and one dressy. Since Alyssa always wore tube socks with her tennies, Kate also had her look at socks that coordinated with the outfits. And she'd need something other than a backpack for the autumn harvest celebration.

They found a small purse that Alyssa oohed over. "Brenda Strong has one just like this!"

"Is she a friend?"

"She's the most popular girl in school," Alyssa explained with a trace of wistfulness. "And she's really pretty."

Kate understood. There were always a few kids the others looked up to. Smiling, she wondered what the other kids would think of Alyssa's makeover. She could hardly wait till morning, when she could come back and buy the shoes, socks and purse. Funny thing, she didn't feel like a fairy godmother. At some elemental level, she guessed it was the joy a genuine mother felt.

The next morning, Kate was up early. She'd told Alyssa the night before that she would be picking up the top and skirt. The rest she intended to smuggle away until the party. Normally, she walked to Main Street, but she'd have too much to carry today.

She stopped first at Mueller's. The party dress looked even prettier than she remembered. She popped open the trunk of the car and stowed the purchases. Then she left the car and walked over to the shoe store. It didn't take long to gather everything on her list.

It was a gorgeous day—true Indian summer. The light would be perfect for working when she got home. Meanwhile, she loved walking the wide, planked sidewalks under the spreading elms. The artist in her connected with the perfect view.

When she was about half a block from her car, she slowed down, recognizing Tucker coming in her direction. She couldn't miss the distinctive stride of his long legs, the squared thrust of broad shoulders. His posture was always ramrod straight, emphasizing his height…his strength. Her hands tightened on the shopping bags. Painfully aware of their contents, she licked her lips and smiled.

Then she saw Turner stop at her car, bending over to examine her taillight. With the engine off, he couldn't tell if she'd replaced the bulb. She'd totally spaced about getting the thing fixed. Even when she grumbled about the ticket, she didn't carry through and find a repair place.

Resisting the urge to turn around and head the other direction, she slowly approached her car. "Morning."

In an old-fashioned but strangely touching manner, he tipped the brim of his hat. "Morning. Saw your car, remembered you're about out of time to bring in the repair receipt."

She fidgeted, hooking one foot behind her

other ankle. "Well…um…I haven't exactly had it fixed yet."

He wrinkled his brow in question.

"What I mean is that it's been so busy, getting Dad settled in, my work…um…and I haven't found a repair place."

"It's only a bulb," he reminded her mildly.

"Just like my dad," she muttered.

"Your *dad?*"

"He thought I ought to be able to bake a pie because it's *just* crust and filling. Never mind that I didn't have a clue how to make either."

"And a taillight bulb falls in the same category—not 'your thing.'"

"Well, yeah." Conscious of the new purchases in the bags she held, Kate clutched them tighter, trying to hide the bags behind her back, failing woefully as they stuck out on both sides. "Thanks for reminding me."

"Want me to open your trunk?" he offered.

The blue party dress was right on top, encased in a clear plastic bag. "Uh, no, that's okay. I'll just stick these inside." She darted to the driver's door and fumbled for the handle, dropping one bag in the process.

He bent to pick it up and she snatched it up first. Realizing it must look as though she was hiding contraband, she tried to relax.

"You a shopaholic?" he quizzed in an amused tone.

"Not really." She reached again for the handle, nearly dropping her purse.

"Let me get that." He opened the door for her.

Nervously, she smiled, then shoved the bags into the passenger seat as she slid inside. "Thanks."

"No problem. And don't worry. I won't tell."

She swallowed, her voice croaky. "Tell what?"

"That you've been shopping. It's not all that bad, you know."

"Oh, right." She nodded, then reached into her purse for her keys.

He tipped his hat again.

As she fitted the key in the ignition, she glanced in the rearview mirror, catching Tucker in her gaze. Tall, muscled, utterly masculine. And realized the perfect view had gotten even better.

The sun was still shining when Tucker finished up and locked the office. But it wouldn't be for much longer. He drove to the Lambert house and pulled into the driveway behind Kate's Jetta. Alyssa would still be at the Lamberts, per their new routine. He reached for the bulb he'd bought at the auto supply store, then into the glove compartment for a screwdriver.

Funny how Kate had been on his mind all day.

In previous encounters, she'd irked, angered and puzzled him, but she'd never made him grin. To himself mostly. And mostly all day.

He wouldn't have taken her for a woman who had a secret shopping obsession—at least he guessed it was. Because he sure didn't think she was smuggling drugs in bags from Barton Shoes. He chuckled to himself. Maybe she already had a closet filled with shoes—another Imelda Marcos.

It didn't take long to remove the red plastic cover on the taillight and replace the bulb. He'd need Kate's keys to turn the car on and make sure the connection was secure and the bulb lit properly. Hearing Alyssa giggle, he peered around the side of the car and saw his daughter skip out the of the kitchen door, Kate right behind her.

"Noodle!" Kate called out.

"Here, kitty, kitty," Alyssa added.

He straightened up, not wanting to look as though he was spying on them.

"Dad!" Alyssa's voice filled with pleasure. As always, the sound warmed him.

"Hey, Pop-tart."

She dashed toward him. "You're home early!"

Kate followed more slowly. "Evening."

He held up the burned-out bulb. "I'll sign off on your ticket now."

"You fixed it?"

"No big deal."

Her brow furrowed. "I didn't expect you to."

He stepped a bit closer. "You didn't invent neighbor helping neighbor."

She looked startled, then flustered. "Of course not." Shoving her hands in the pockets of her jeans, she seemed, for once, at a loss for words.

"Guess what we made?" Alyssa was practically dancing in her tennies. "Fried chicken! Your favorite!"

"Alyssa tried to teach me, but luckily she cooked the chicken." Kate shook her head, then paused. "Where are my manners? We'll set another plate. Daisy's joining us—Mrs. Ford, that is."

His voice was mild. "I know her."

She thumped her forehead, a light motion. "Of course you do…." Her voice trailed off.

"It's okay," Alyssa assured her. "You haven't lived here long enough to know who knows who."

Kate gave her a small hug. A genuine one, Tucker noted. "And I'm kind of frazzled today." She glanced at him. "Why don't you come inside and wash up? I think the biscuits should be done. Since all I had to do was pop open the wrapper and stick them in the oven, they should be safe."

Marvin and Daisy greeted him with big smiles. Daisy added a hug to her greeting. He hadn't realized how much he'd missed his neighbors. Shutting himself off, he'd lost the comfort and support of friends, people he'd known all his life.

Still, he felt awkward sitting with the group in the dining room. But Marvin acted as though Tucker ate with them every night. The round table was spacious enough to easily accommodate them, but small enough to make the setting intimate. Alyssa sat between Kate and him. Daisy was on his other side and Marvin's wheelchair was positioned so that he could easily reach the table.

After Marvin blessed the food, he offered Tucker the platter of chicken. Daisy started the mashed potatoes, then passed them on.

"I made the gravy," Alyssa confided as she ladled some onto her potatoes.

Tucker accepted the bowl of mashed potatoes. "It looks great."

Alyssa nodded. "It should all be good. Kate only did the biscuits."

Embarrassed and slightly horrified, Tucker stared at his daughter. "*Alyssa!* That's no way to talk."

Kate waved her hands, then pulled a mock grimace. "It's okay. She's right."

Tucker looked at Kate. She'd taken the comment easily, but the slight bothered him. Kate always acted confident, but he'd seen brief lapses of vulnerability. "Still, Lissy…"

"Sorry, Dad." Abashed, she glanced up at Kate. "I didn't mean anything by it."

Kate patted her arm. "I know you didn't. Hanging around with you and Daisy, I'm picking up bits here and there, but I don't think cooking's something I'm ever going to excel at."

"I like you just the way you are," Marvin declared. "Not taking away from Daisy and Alyssa's talents, you're a renowned art restorer. How many people can say that?"

Kate blushed, a mild, pinkish glow that Tucker found oddly endearing.

"Not many," Daisy seconded. "Your father has good reason to be so proud of you."

Tucker had known Daisy and her husband since he was a boy. He respected her opinion. Her words made him wonder even more about Kate— what laid beneath her oft-changing expression.

Kate cleared her throat. "Careful, or all this will go to my head." Affection filled her eyes as she looked first at her father, then Daisy. "So, what about this fried chicken?"

Everyone chimed in, agreeing that it was delicious. Tucker noticed that Kate discreetly patted Alyssa's arm again, smiling warmly. He'd been crucially aware that his daughter missed and needed a mother's attention. But watching her now, it hit hard.

Although he was quiet, Tucker listened to the others as the leisurely dinner progressed. Daisy's German chocolate cake topped off the meal, and he realized he'd eaten more than he usually did in a day.

Marvin patted his stomach. "I'm stuffed."

Kate began clearing the table and Daisy immediately stood. "Let Alyssa and me do this."

"But—"

"No buts," Daisy insisted. "I know Alyssa's finished her homework and you've put in a long day."

Kate looked uncertain, so Tucker spoke up. "I still have to check the taillight. Make sure the bulb works. I'll need your keys."

"Looks like I'm outnumbered," Kate conceded, setting down the plate she held.

"Go on, dear," Daisy advised, as she took charge of the cleanup. "And start your car for Tucker."

Kate disappeared for a minute, returning with her keys. "Noodle's still outside. Better make sure he comes in."

The air was crisp in the early evening darkness. Despite the warm day, the heat had receded, leaving the night temperate, calming.

"I feel pretty stupid about this taillight ticket thing," Kate admitted, as they approached her car.

"No need to," he replied, surprising himself. Initially, he'd dismissed her as irresponsible. Now he was excusing her. He opened the driver's side door.

Her expression was difficult to read as she glanced up at him, pausing before she slid inside. "Thanks."

The wind sighed lightly, ruffling the trees, eliciting the fragrance of late-blooming roses. Overhead, the half moon reflected off the rooftops, danced over the cobblestone street.

Tucker tried to ignore the lure of the night, concentrating instead on the job at hand. "Turn the lights on."

She complied. As expected, the taillight lit up.

"Turn them off and hit the brakes."

Again, it worked.

She poked her head out from the car. "Is it okay?"

Her face was soft in the muted moonlight. Tucker cleared his throat. "Yeah."

She sighed in relief as she stood. "I really appreciate this. I should have had it repaired before now."

"You've been busy."

Kate toed the tip of her sandal against the driveway. "I was mad about the ticket."

His brow furrowed. "Still?"

"No." She hesitated. "But I could have made time to get the bulb replaced. I just…"

He smiled to himself. "I've felt the same way about some things. You're frosted about what happened, so it's not easy to deal with."

She nodded, then looked down at her shoes. "We got off to a pretty bad start, didn't we?"

"I imagine you had a life back in the city. Gave it up to come take care of your father. Couldn't have been easy."

Kate lifted her gaze, and he saw the unique color of her eyes deepen. He also saw that fleeting vulnerability, along with pain. It disappeared as quickly as it had appeared, but he had seen it. "My family's everything to me—small as it is. When you shake that down, it wasn't hard to know what I had to do…what I wanted to do. I suppose I didn't think anything else was important."

"Not even a ticket from a small-town sheriff?" he teased gently.

Her laugh was soft, quiet. "I'm not going to live that one down, am I?"

"Doubtful."

Tilting her head back, she looked up at the star-filled sky. "Ah. Never realized how inspiring sleepy, small towns can be."

He looked at the slim column of her neck, her pale skin glistening, the curve of her throat as it arched.

Inspiring....

It had been a lifetime since he'd stood in the moonlight next to a woman. A lifetime forever unwound.

Chapter Nine

Kate glanced at her watch, then tapped Alyssa's hand. "We'd better hurry!"

The clerk rang up the magazines they'd bought in the drugstore and they hurried out and down the sidewalk. Over milkshakes at the marble fountain, Kate and Alyssa had been studying teen style magazines, trying to find a hairstyle that suited the girl.

"Dad always takes me with him to the barber," Alyssa said tentatively. "And my mom used to cut my hair. Is it different at a salon?"

"Same principle. But your hair'll turn out more like when your Mom cut it."

Alyssa smiled softly. "That'd be cool."

Kate felt the tug on her heart. No outward makeover could ever match the beauty of this child's soul. She placed an arm over Alyssa's shoulders as they walked the last few blocks. Once inside, Alyssa looked nervous as she clutched the page she'd torn from a magazine.

"There's nothing to be scared about," Kate whispered in her ear. "And I'll be right here the whole time."

Alyssa slipped her other hand into Kate's.

When it was their turn, Kate rose with Alyssa and walked over to the stylist chair. "Alyssa's brought a picture of what she likes. Can you tell us if it'll work with her hair?"

With Alyssa seated, the attractive stylist, Beth, ran her fingers through the dark, shiny hair. "Thick, supple." Beth met Alyssa's eyes in the mirror across from the chair. "With your bone structure, you'll look pretty in most any cut."

Snipping skillfully, Beth created layers and transformed the jagged bangs. When she finished cutting, she added mousse, then picked up a blow-dryer. "You can style your hair in just a couple of minutes. Towel dry, add your product." The youngish woman held up the mousse so Alyssa could see it. "Then blow-dry. It's pretty foolproof." Alyssa looked intrigued and she watched carefully as Beth styled her dark hair.

When Beth was done, Alyssa stared in the mirror, her voice shocked. "It looks so different."

"I told you you'd look pretty in any style." Beth grinned, clearly pleased.

Alyssa spun around. "What do you think, Kate?"

Touched that Alyssa cared so much about her opinion, Kate swallowed the knot of emotion. "You look lovely."

"Nah." Alyssa's eyes darted to the floor, then back up shyly.

Kate stroked the girl's soft hair. "Yes. Lovely."

Tucker felt the beginning of a migraine. He'd never had one before Shelley died. The doctor said they were most likely triggered by stress. Dealing with work, not dealing as well as he should with Alyssa—the cause of his stress was a no-brainer. He'd promised himself he'd get home early. Tucker glanced at his watch as he got out of the truck. Well, it was ten minutes earlier than usual.

The house smelled good. Alyssa was cooking. Even though he wasn't crazy about the amount of time she was spending at the Lamberts, he knew it was better than her coming home to an empty house.

He thought about Kate as he'd stood with her in the moonlight earlier in the week. Feeling guilty, he wondered if Shelley would approve of the woman Alyssa was spending so much time with. His heart empty, he tried not to grimace as he entered the bright light of the kitchen. He took off his hat and hung it on the peg. "Lissy?"

"Hey, Dad," she hollered from the living room. Funny, he didn't hear the television.

"Smells good." He wasn't hungry, but he wasn't going to disappoint his daughter.

She scooted into the kitchen, her feet in socks, sliding to a stop. "I did that potato and cheese dish you like. And there's ham from yesterday."

He dropped a kiss on the top of her head. "How'd you get this together so fast?"

"Last night I got the potatoes ready and just now baked it. And I stuck the ham in the oven to warm while the potatoes were cooking." She shrugged. "No big deal."

The light was killing his head. "How 'bout we carry our plates into the living room, maybe watch a movie while we eat."

"Okay. What do you want to see?"

"Why don't you pick, honey."

She scrunched her face into questioning lines. "Are you okay?"

"Sure."

"You don't *look* okay."

Tucker turned away so she couldn't study his face. "I'll go wash up."

In the bathroom, he found the aspirin and downed two. Lately, they hadn't helped enough, but he didn't want to take the strong medication the doctor had suggested. He couldn't do his job, either as sheriff or a parent, all drugged up.

After washing his hands, he splashed his face with cool water.

Alyssa had the food and plates out on the counter when he got back to the kitchen.

"You want a big slice of ham?" she asked, carving the meat.

"Just average."

She sliced another piece, then put one on each plate.

Tucker opened the refrigerator. "What do you want to drink?"

"I've got some milk in the living room," she replied, scooping potatoes on each plate.

He reached for a soda, having found the caffeine, along with the aspirin, helped his headache more.

Alyssa popped a DVD in the player, then settled next to him on the couch. He was glad she kept the volume low. The potatoes were tasty, and she'd snuck in some cauliflower, which actually tasted okay. "It's really good, Lissy."

She ducked her head a fraction as she smiled. There was something about her… Tucker's head throbbed. He couldn't place it, but she looked different somehow. Although he didn't want it, he gamely cut his ham and ate a bite.

"Dad…um, you know how I have a book report due?"

He tried to remember. "I thought you just did one."

"That was for fiction. Now I have to do one on a biography." She paused. "I thought I'd ask Kate if I could practice it on her this week."

He put down his fork. "Can't you practice it for me?"

"Well…I guess…it's just that there's not that much time…." Her voice trailed away.

But he knew what she meant. They were already eating dinner late every night. By the time she could practice, it'd be her bedtime. "It's fine, Lissy. I know I haven't caught up with my work enough to get home early."

Her eyes filled with concern. "I didn't mean to make you feel bad, Daddy."

She hadn't called him that in a long while. "You didn't." He swallowed his injured pride. "It's good Kate can help you."

"There's one more thing…."

Tucker wondered if his head might explode like a punctured balloon. "Yes?"

"You know the autumn harvest celebration? The one at school, I mean. Can I go?"

He thought for a moment. The celebration was a safe event. The kids got together in the gym, had refreshments and games. "I don't see why not."

A grin exploded on her face. She plunked her plate on the coffee table and reached over to hug him. "Thanks, Daddy!"

"Whoa, what's all this?" He couldn't remember her getting so excited by a school event since she was a little thing.

She shook her head. "Nothing. Just…my… friends'll be there, and it'll be lots of fun."

Fun. He hadn't provided any of that for his child since Shelley died. "Good. I'm sorry I've neglected that, too."

She hugged him again. "Don't worry, Daddy. It's going to be all right."

Words he should be saying to her. But he didn't have the conviction to utter them.

A few days later, Kate and Alyssa dawdled in the makeup section of the drugstore. They'd found a barely pink lip gloss that suited Alyssa. Now they were examining the selection of nail polish.

"I like this one." Kate held up a pale pink that was close to the color of the gloss they'd settled on.

Alyssa tilted her head, studying the bottle, then she reached for another one. "This one's a little lighter." It had a soft, iridescent shimmer.

"Which do you like better?"

"The lighter one, I think."

As Kate collected emery boards and cuticle sticks, an unfamiliar woman approached. Glancing up, Kate realized at once the woman was a tourist. It hadn't taken her long to acquire the knack. Lettered T-shirt, camera around her neck, hat and unfortunate Bermuda shorts.

"Excuse me," the woman began, slipping off her sunglasses. "I'm looking for some postcards. Do you know where I can find some?"

Kate shook her head. "We don't have any souvenir shops."

"And this drugstore doesn't carry any?" she asked, surprised.

"Afraid not. Rosewood just isn't a touristy place."

"But it's so lovely!" The woman looked almost desolate.

Kate remained silent, rather than sound rude saying what she thought—that the town was lovely because the residents had resisted going the tourist route.

The woman sighed. "That's too bad." She glanced at Alyssa. "Your daughter's sure a cutie. Bye now."

Kate glanced at Alyssa, hoping her feelings hadn't been hurt. "She just made an assumption."

"It's okay." Alyssa's eyes darted to the floor.

Kate gave her a small hug. "I'm craving chocolate."

"We could make some brownies," Alyssa offered.

Kate groaned. "You're good for me, not so much for my willpower." She grabbed a box of macadamia chocolates that were made locally. "This'll do."

Kate paid and they strolled out onto Main Street. "You never did tell me—what did your dad think of your new haircut?"

She stubbed one tennis shoe against the pavement. "He hasn't exactly noticed."

Kate held in her dismay. "He must have work on his mind. He had an awful lot of paperwork in his office the time I was there."

"Yeah. He doesn't mean to be late and stuff…."

Kate's throat tightened. She wondered what it would take for Tucker to get past his grief.

Back at the house, Marvin and Alyssa playfully argued over the chocolates. It was gratifying to watch as her father's relationship with the girl progressed. Emma was right. He *should* have grandchildren. But she wouldn't trade Alyssa for anyone else. The thought was sobering. Only one thing was missing—a husband.

Since she had broken up with Derek, she'd reexamined her relationship with him. Initially, she'd been hurt; but Kate found she didn't miss his lack of sensitivity, his self-absorption. Her father and the few new friends she'd made seemed more interested in her than Derek ever had. Strange how she hadn't seen that, hadn't realized how wrong he was for her.

The afternoon seemed to fly by as they painted fingernails, then toenails. Manicures complete, they were admiring their work when the doorbell rang. Kate glanced at the clock. "Good grief! It's nearly six. Without Dad and Daisy here, I completely lost track of time." The duo were at Daisy's, where she was teaching Marvin how to make her sticky buns. The thought made her grin. Mr. Barbecue was going to bake.

Kate hurried to the door when the bell rang again.

Tucker looked concerned.

So Kate held up her newly polished nails. "Sorry. I was just finishing up—didn't want to spill the nail polish."

He shifted uncomfortably, clearly not a guy who knew or cared about manicures. Not surprising. He was all man from his dark hair that begged to be tousled to the rigid soles of his cowboy boots.

Alyssa popped out beside her. "Hey, Dad."

His expression warmed as he looked at his

daughter. "Did you start dinner yet? Thought you might like to eat at the café."

"Can Kate come? Her dad and Daisy aren't here, and so nothing's cooking."

Tucker looked distinctly uncomfortable.

"You don't have to invite me." Feeling much like the girl no one asks to the party, Kate tried to act nonplussed. "I can grab a sandwich."

"We want to, don't we, Dad?" Alyssa smiled up her father.

He didn't meet Kate's eyes. "Sure."

Not exactly a winsome invitation. But Alyssa looked expectant. "I could use a warm dinner." And the company of a certain sheriff, even if he had to be coaxed a bit.

Tucker kept his eyes on the road as he drove to Main Street, since Kate was sitting beside him. Alyssa had conveniently hopped in the back, leaving the passenger seat in the front empty. Glancing over, he noticed that Kate didn't look real comfortable either.

Since the evening he'd fixed her taillight, he'd been assailed by guilt. Sure, he'd noticed Kate since she'd come to town. She wasn't easily ignored. But he didn't want to resurrect any of the emotions he buried with Shelley.

He'd vowed never to get involved with anyone else. And until Kate came along, it had been easy to keep his promise. Somehow, Kate had insinuated herself into their lives so seamlessly that he wasn't even sure how she'd managed it.

He pulled into one of the angled parking spaces in front of the café.

Once inside, Alyssa headed straight for their favorite booth, a curved one at the back of the room. She slid into the booth first.

Unable to disregard his manners, he gestured for Kate to sit before he did, which put them side-by-side.

Alyssa passed around the menus that had been tucked behind the napkin holder.

With Kate's city experience, he imagined she found the menu lacking.

"Ooh," Kate murmured.

"Something wrong?"

"They've got fresh fish tonight! How am I supposed to choose between that and the chicken-fried steak?"

Not what he expected. But then, he hadn't expected to be sitting next to her again. Although she *had* scooted in as close as possible to the other side. But the booth, designed for only two or three people, didn't give her much extra space.

Kate kept her eyes down on the menu, but

Tucker didn't believe she was all that fascinated with the selection.

"Dad, are we going to have pie here, or go for ice cream?" Alyssa asked.

"What if you're too full for dessert?"

"I'm planning so I won't be."

He didn't want to draw out the evening. "Let's wait and see how you feel after dinner."

Alyssa had always loved the homemade macaroni and cheese, which she ordered. Kate finally settled on the fish. "I'll get the steak next time, Della." The waitress scribbled their requests.

Tucker didn't particularly care what he ate, but automatically ordered meat loaf. It reminded him of his mother's.

"That sounds good, too." Kate looked torn.

Surprised, he lifted his eyebrows. "Not a very sophisticated palate, for a city person."

"I wasn't raised in the middle of the business district. We lived way out in the suburbs, had a yard and everything. Left to my own devices, I eat TV dinners and sandwiches."

Alyssa rolled her eyes. "Just like Dad."

He cleared his throat.

Kate looked away.

"What?" Alyssa asked.

"Nothing," he replied. Kate lifted her eyes and he saw her instant understanding.

The moment stretched out.

Glancing down, he saw her newly polished nails, remembered the feel of her hand in his. He shifted, but there was no place for him to retreat, either.

Della returned with their glasses of iced tea. Relieved to have something to do with his hands, he added sugar, then offered the dispenser to Kate.

She waved it away. "I like it plain." But she busied her hands with the quarter of lemon, devoting more attention to the task than necessary.

Any more tension in the confined space and they could generate electricity.

When the waitress returned with a basket of fresh rolls and wedges of cornbread, they reached at the same time for the bread. Although his hand only grazed hers, he was painfully conscious that it felt exactly as he remembered.

"Bread's always been my downfall," Kate chattered. "When it's good like this, I eat too much, then I'm too full for my entree, not to mention dessert. Well, sometimes I'll eat dessert anyway." She smiled too brightly. "Most of the time, actually."

Alyssa looked at her strangely but didn't say anything.

Kate concentrated on buttering her roll as though she were restoring a priceless piece of art.

"Don't you feel good?" Alyssa asked him.

Tucker straightened up to an even stiffer posture. "I'm fine."

"Hmm." Alyssa didn't look convinced.

And Kate continued to fiddle with her roll, even though it was already buttered.

"You want extra gravy on your potatoes, Tucker?" Della asked, startling him.

He managed not to jump. "Sure."

"Won't be long." Della looked around the table. "Need anything right now?"

"No," he and Kate replied in unison.

Della's eyebrows shot up. "Okay, then."

"I love the way the café always has fresh flowers on every table." Kate touched the small ceramic vase. "I even like the vases. Looks handcrafted. Let me guess, the potter lives right here in Rosewood."

"Not anymore."

She adjusted the vase so she could see the other side. "I didn't think anyone left this town."

"Technically he didn't." Tucker picked up his glass. "He's in the cemetery."

Kate froze, then drew her hand back.

Della arrived with their meals. Next to him, he felt the gentle swish of breath leave Kate. Apparently as relieved as he was.

Tucker knew why he was relieved. But he wondered why Kate was.

Chapter Ten

Kate picked up a small brush, then glanced out the window. She hadn't been able to get the evening at the café out of her thoughts. Something had gotten under Tucker's skin. Kate just wasn't sure what. It seemed all the progress they'd made had disappeared. Of course, he could be worried about work. Or a million other things. But she suspected it was personal.

She hadn't told Alyssa about the clothes and shoes she'd bought for her, so it couldn't be that. In fact, she planned the surprise for that afternoon. Kate was anxious as she waited for Alyssa to get out of school.

But it was worth the wait.

Tentatively, Alyssa touched the blue dress, then the sweater. She whirled around. "You bought them *all!* And you matched up all the shoes, socks and stuff…." Alyssa's expression went from shock to pleasure to disbelief.

Realizing she was overwhelmed, Kate tucked a wisp of hair behind Alyssa's ear. "I'm sure your dad would have bought you these things if he'd known he was supposed to. But men are kind of clueless about clothes, you know?"

Alyssa nodded, but tears shone in her eyes.

Kate leaned forward and hugged the child, knowing Alyssa must be making the mental leap to what else she was missing out on, without a mother. "Not having children of my own, I haven't been able to do this before."

"Are you ever going to have kids?"

Bittersweet emotion swamped her and she had to clear her throat. "I don't know," she answered truthfully. Knowing she had to lighten the mood, Kate smiled. "So, what do you think you're going to wear for the big night?"

"Wow." Alyssa looked at the assortment. "Will you help me decide?"

Kate ruffled Alyssa's hair, barely willing to trust her own voice. "Wait till Donny Kimball sees you."

Alyssa looked suddenly uncertain. "I wish you could be there."

"Well…"

"What?" Alyssa shifted from side to side as though about to burst. "What?"

"I talked to Emma and found out how to volunteer to be a chaperone. So…"

Alyssa leaped up and threw her arms around Kate's neck.

And Kate's heart expanded in a way it never had before.

The afternoon of the festival, Alyssa called to remind Tucker again that the harvest celebration was that night. When he didn't answer, she left a voice mail, asking him to call her back.

Kate checked the time. "Since it's Friday, with people going out of town for the weekend, the highway could be busy. And noisy, I imagine. He might not be able to hear his phone."

Alyssa's face crumpled.

"What is it, honey?"

"I can't go if Dad doesn't know it's tonight."

Kate thought for a moment. "You definitely asked him for permission?"

Eyes miserable, the girl nodded.

"And you mentioned it to him this afternoon when you first called to check in?"

"Uh-huh."

Kate mulled this over. She couldn't stand the thought of Alyssa missing the party because of a communications snafu. She also didn't believe that Tucker would want Alyssa to miss the much-anticipated event. "I'll call his office and cell and leave a message that I'll take you."

By sunset, Alyssa was dressed and ready. Shyly, she entered the living room.

Marvin feigned lack of recognition. "Who's this?" He turned to his daughter. "Kate, we have a beautiful young girl here. You didn't tell me we were having company."

Alyssa giggled. "It's me."

He narrowed his eyes as though in deep thought. "Sounds like Alyssa. What do you think, Kate?"

"I think you're right. It's our beautiful Ally."

The girl's eyes darted to the floor, then she looked up shyly. "Do I really look okay?"

"More than okay," Kate confirmed.

"My dad still hasn't called. Are you sure we can go?"

"Your dad wouldn't want you to miss your party," Kate assured her. Surely Tucker would understand the situation.

When they arrived at the school, lots of other students and parents were also streaming inside. Alyssa shook with excitement as they walked inside. Red, orange and yellow crepe paper, along with balloons, hung from the rafters. Corn husks and bales of hay transformed the gym to a cozy barn-like setting. Games were set up across the wide expanse, and some of the kids had begun playing them.

But plenty of girls were bunched together, talking and giggling. Nearly as many boys stood in groups as well, trying to look grownup, hoping they didn't look nervous. Kate smiled at the twang of nerves and excitement that danced in the air.

Emma was already in place, manning the buffet table, and they walked across the gym to stand by her. Lots of parents were in attendance, and as promised, Kate blended in with them.

She leaned close to Alyssa so she could whisper. "Do you see him?"

Alyssa blushed, a soft pink that only enhanced her cute face. "He's over there," she whispered, pointing with just the barest tip of one finger. "He has blond hair and he's wearing a blue shirt," Alyssa added furtively.

Kate spotted the boy. He was talking to friends, but he wasn't adopting a false swagger. She hoped he was as nice as he appeared.

Since everyone was welcoming, Kate felt at ease, but she didn't believe Alyssa was. Every few minutes, she tugged at her skirt or sleeves.

Kate didn't want to push, but she knew that,

while Alyssa stuck to her side, she wouldn't venture much farther. She leaned close, her voice quiet. "Go on, honey. Join your friends."

Alyssa swallowed, clearly torn.

"Trust me. It'll be okay."

Dread and anticipation clashed in Alyssa's face. Then she took a breath, clutched her new purse, and walked toward her friends. Kate felt like a mother hen as she watched their reactions. As she'd expected, the girls surrounded Alyssa, exclaiming over her new dress and accessories. Some of her friends had commented on her hair the day after she'd had it cut, but, combined with all the other changes, it was a startling transformation. No longer boyish and unkempt, Alyssa was a pretty preteen girl. Nothing racy or inappropriate—just what suited her.

Not wanting to make Alyssa self-conscious by hovering too close, Kate turned back to the buffet table, fiddling with a cup of punch.

"Can I make you a plate?" Emma offered.

"Are you kidding? I'm too nervous to eat. I just hope Donny notices."

Emma grinned. "She looks great. You did good."

"Combined effort. Thanks for all the advice."

"Like I told you, it's sort of a tradition in Rosewood. Since I was once a newcomer, it's my turn to make things easier for you." She straightened a stack of napkins. "What does Tucker think of all the changes?"

"He hasn't seen the clothes yet…." Kate sighed. "But he didn't notice Alyssa's hair."

Emma's eyes filled with sympathy. "He hasn't seen much of anything for two years. Losing Shelley broke him. But poor Alyssa…."

"She's remarkable. Defends him no matter what."

"You don't approve?"

"It's not that." Kate vividly remembered her own behavior when she'd lost her mother. "I know why she champions him. And I understand how hurt Tucker is. But my dad was always there for me. She needs that kind of support, too."

Emma's eyes darkened, then she looked away. "It's not easy being the survivor."

Kate jerked her head upward, hating that she'd hurt her friend. "Emma, please know that's not what I meant. I can't even imagine how you coped."

"Lots of prayer, even more faith."

Kate swallowed, her throat tight. "And you've brought that back into my life."

Emma smiled. "I just nudged." She glanced up. "Look! Isn't that Donny Kimball with Alyssa?"

Kate turned, remembering how it felt to be

that age, to have your first crush. Full of butter-flies, she studied Alyssa and Donny. Inconspicuously, she hoped.

The duo strolled slowly to the punch table. Donny scooped punch first for Alyssa, then for himself. They were so cute, she could have burst. Instead, she made herself stop the intense surveillance. "Emma, do you just want to melt when you see your kids doing something cute?"

"All the time. When Toby's playing with the twins…" She paused. "You know his life at that age wasn't very good. But he adores the babies, plays with them, spoils them. I'm guessing you've had a few melting moments yourself lately?"

"Can't help it. Alyssa's so unspoiled, and she's amazingly thoughtful." Kate turned back to Emma. "I was close to my dad at that age, but I didn't take care of him the way…" Hearing raised voices, her words trailed away, shocked to recognize Tucker's loud voice. Seeing that he had cornered Donny, Kate rushed to the other side of the gym.

"I asked you what you think you're doing!" Tucker demanded, gripping Donny's arm.

The terrified boy didn't speak.

Kate pushed herself between them, forcing Tucker to release Donny. "What do you think *you're* doing?" she hissed, pushing Donny behind her.

The boy stared at Tucker from his relatively safe position. Everyone else in the gym had stopped talking and were staring as well.

"Alyssa is *my* daughter," Tucker retorted. He held out his hand. "Come on, Alyssa."

Shaking her head, Alyssa broke into tears, then ran off, pushing open the double doors that led outside.

"What do you think you're doing?" Tucker demanded of Kate. "Dressing up my child, taking it on yourself to bring her here without asking me?" His voice was loud, echoing through the space, seeming to ricochet from the bleachers to the rafters.

Realizing he didn't know how much he'd over-reacted and unwilling to have this discussion in front of the gaping crowd, Kate didn't answer. Instead, she left to search for Alyssa. She could hear Tucker barely a foot behind her, but she didn't look back. He clearly needed help, but dealing with Alyssa was foremost. She didn't see the girl in the parking lot. Was she walking home?

"What do you—"

"Shush!" Kate hissed. "Do you hear that?"

The faint sound of crying reached them. Kate looked toward the grassy area to her left and loped in that direction. Beneath one of the tall, sheltering trees, Alyssa was crumpled into a sobbing heap.

"Lissy…" Tucker began.

She cried even harder.

Kate knelt next to Alyssa and smoothed back the hair on her forehead. "It's going to be all right, honey."

Alyssa's tear-streaked face was puffy and red. "Nuh-uh."

Tucker shifted awkwardly as he reached in his pocket for a handkerchief, but his voice had gentled. "Lissy, we'll go home and—"

"No!" She ignored his outstretched hand. Her lips trembled and more tears coursed down her cheeks. "I don't want to go home with you!"

Eyes wide, his voice filled with dumbfounded pain. "Lissy, you don't mean that."

"Yes I do!"

Kate continued smoothing the girl's hair. "Everything will be all right. Just remember what your mother told you."

Tucker looked even more shocked.

Alyssa grasped Kate's hand. "Don't leave, please."

Helplessly, Kate stared at the girl, then Tucker.

"I want to go live with Grandma and Grandpa," Alyssa blurted out between gulping cries. "Away from here."

Tucker's face paled. Shaken, he stared at his child.

His pain was so apparent that Kate wanted to cry for them both. She remembered Alyssa mentioning her grandparents, who lived in Dallas. The separation would be wrenching for both Tucker and Alyssa.

Kate continued to hold the child's hand, but met Tucker's gaze with a powerful one of her own. "I think your dad will agree that he over-reacted tonight."

He opened his mouth.

She shot him a look he couldn't fail interpreting.

And he closed his mouth, lips thinning.

"Right, Tucker?"

Clearly, he wanted to object. But he looked at Alyssa, who hadn't stopping crying and was still hanging on to Kate. "I guess so."

"Everything's all ruined!" Alyssa wailed.

"No, it's not," Kate insisted. "Your dad will talk to Donny and his parents. It'll be okay." She wondered if she'd pushed one step too far when his brow furrowed and his eyes narrowed. "Okay, Ally?"

Reluctantly, Alyssa nodded a fraction.

"Your dad loves you very much." Kate took the handkerchief from Tucker and gave it to the girl. "You're the most important thing in the world to him."

Alyssa sniffled and Tucker shifted restlessly. Kate didn't need to see his face to know he resented her taking control of the situation.

"So," Kate continued, "maybe it would be best to go home for the evening. You'll see Donny at school and church."

"She's too young—" Tucker began.

"Alyssa knows she's far too young to date, but she'd like Donny to be her friend." Kate met his gaze, her own unflinching. "And none of us can have too many of those, can we?"

Whatever Tucker was thinking, wisely, he didn't voice it.

"Why don't I walk home with you?" Kate suggested. "Seems like some hot cocoa wouldn't go amiss."

Alyssa still clinging to Kate, they walked toward home. Over the child's head, Kate signaled caution with her expression. And prayed he would treat the night gently. And show the love he'd held in for his daughter.

Chapter Eleven

Treading lightly, Tucker tried to make amends with Alyssa. She wasn't mad. Worse, she was hurt and disappointed. His behavior had humiliated her in front of all her friends, something she didn't think could be fixed. He still couldn't believe it had come to this.

The morning after the disastrous autumn harvest celebration, he tried to talk to her. But the entire time, she looked as though she was about to cry. So he'd allowed her to go to Kate's for the day.

Feeling more alone than he'd ever been in his life, he wandered into Alyssa's room after she left. Neatly hung in her closet were clothes he'd never seen before. Her T-shirts and overalls were still there, making the comparison pitiful. Sitting next to her extra pair of tennis shoes, he saw new shoes as well.

On top of the dresser, she'd arranged some barrettes, along with nail polish and some sort of lipstick. He still thought of Alyssa as his baby. Had he been so shuttered in his grief that he'd missed the changes in her?

He assumed Kate had bought all the new things. Apparently, she understood more about his daughter than he did. Now he couldn't stop wondering if all this had been right in front of him. Alyssa had never complained, never asked for anything. And that made him feel even worse.

She'd barely spoken since Friday night. At least to him. She'd gone to church the day before, then come home and stayed in her room. Now she was at school.

Tucker wasn't used to asking for help. He'd never gone to a counselor. Before Shelley's death, his counsel had been his minister, but that wasn't an option any longer. Still, he needed someone to talk to.

He glanced at his watch. Eight o'clock Monday morning. With the pit in his stomach growing, he called Kate and asked if she had some time to talk. His deputy, Owen, had agreed to man the office.

A few weeks ago, he'd hoped to get his life back on track, be a good father. And now he just hoped he hadn't lost Alyssa.

* * *

Kate had agreed to ten o'clock. He stayed on patrol until the last possible second. His footsteps lagged as he climbed the steps of the Lambert front porch. He hated that he needed to talk to Kate about Alyssa. But he would do anything to repair this tear in their relationship.

Within moments of ringing the bell, Kate opened the door. "Come in. How 'bout some coffee?"

He took off his hat and nodded.

She reached for his hat and placed it on the coatrack in the entry. "Noodle has a way of destroying hats."

"Noodle?"

She chuckled. "My cat. I forget it's not a common pet name, since I'm used to it. You remember him? From…" she paused. "The day I moved here."

It was hard to forget. If he hadn't been so grumpy at the time, he'd have laughed at the sight of Kate's cat attached to her head like a coonskin cap.

"He usually hides when we have company, so you probably haven't seen him since our escapade on Main Street." Kate led the way into the kitchen. "Dad's over at Daisy's. They play Scrabble every day now." She grabbed a mug and filled it with fresh-smelling coffee. "Cream or sugar?"

"Just black."

She handed him his coffee, then poured a mug for herself. She carried it over to the table. "This okay? I think kitchens are friendlier."

"Fine with me."

"I know this isn't easy for you." She pursed her lips, hesitated. "I hope you know how much I care for Alyssa, too."

Even though it had been his idea to talk, he didn't want to lay his soul bare for anyone. "Good coffee."

"Yes, well…" Kate cleared her throat. "Alyssa told me that you lost your wife about two years ago."

The shaft of pain he lived with dug a fraction deeper. He hated talking about Shelley's death, just as much as he loved and missed her. "Yeah."

"Do you want to tell me about it?"

No. He wanted to get back on a steady footing with Alyssa. "She died. Cancer."

Her eyes gentled, understanding filling them. "I'm sure it's hard for you to talk about it."

Despite her empathy, he clenched his jaw. "Yeah."

Kate leaned back, took a sip of her coffee. "Can you tell me how you met her?"

Surprised, the unreasonable resentment lessened. "I don't see how talking about that is going to help me with Alyssa."

"I'm just trying to find a place to start." She curled her fingers around the coffee mug. "I'll be honest. I was surprised you didn't pick an old friend to talk with."

He could have, despite the fact that he'd avoided all of them. They weren't the kind of people to hold that against him. But none of them had spent the amount of time with Alyssa that Kate had. "Lissy trusts you."

Kate listened silently.

"And I haven't really talked to any of my friends since…" He picked up his mug, then set it down without taking a sip. "This is about her, not me."

"I think it's about you both," she replied softly.

He stared down at the oak table. "She took her first steps on my birthday. Next to the day she was born, it was the best present I ever had."

Before he knew her intention, she covered his hand with her smaller, softer one. "She still is. What you've gone through together…well, I know from experience it makes you closer. But it makes Alyssa more vulnerable, too."

Kate's skin was as silky as he remembered, her touch as intriguing. "Enough to make her want to leave."

"I truly, truly believe you'll get through this." Kate hesitated. "When my mother died, I thought the world had ended. But my dad stayed so strong...made me believe we'd be okay. I think Alyssa needs that same sort of reassurance."

If her eyes weren't so filled with understanding, he would have been angered by her assumption. "And you think I don't do that?"

"In your own way." She leaned forward. "I'm not trying to upset you, but Alyssa's on shaky ground right now. She depends on you to make her world safe, and now..."

"It's not." He tilted his head back, unable to believe he kept all of Rosewood feeling safe except his daughter.

"She's at such a vulnerable age." Kate paused. "I can remember how uncertain I was at twelve. I was lucky, though. I had two aunts and the lady next door to talk to."

If possible, he felt even worse. "And Alyssa's just got me?"

"I didn't mean it that way!" she hastened to assure him. "Just that by closing out your old friends, Alyssa doesn't have a network of support. The day you came to the church picnic she was so happy. I didn't know her that well then, but it was obvious."

"Church isn't an option." He knew his voice was blunt, the words clipped, but this wasn't a point he would negotiate.

Kate bit down on her lip. Then she picked up her mug, sipping her coffee.

Impatiently, he waited for her to say something. Silence.

He tapped his fingers on the table.

Kate still didn't speak.

"What?" he finally asked.

"What's more important? Holding your grudge? Or Alyssa?"

"Grudge?"

"Against the Lord," she replied calmly. "You're not exactly the first person who's blamed God for losing the one they love."

He stared at her, anger stirring him. "You don't have a clue."

"I know you don't want to lose Alyssa. It's going to take more than just telling her you love her. You're going to have to make some changes." She held up her hand. "Right now you're thinking I'm a buttinsky, that I don't know what I'm talking about." She shrugged. "I don't have all the answers. I'm not going to pretend I do. But I do know you and Alyssa belong together."

"If I get over my grudge?"

"When I moved here, I hadn't been inside a church in years. I hadn't stopped believing. I'd just drifted away. But, you know something? The Lord didn't hold it against me. If I hadn't reconnected, I couldn't keep believing my dad would be okay…" Her lips trembled. "I was terrified that I'd lose him." She swiped at her eyes and he saw the start of tears she quickly brushed away.

"Marvin's strong as a horse." Suddenly awkward, Tucker found himself in the position of comforting her. "Anybody can look at him and see that."

Kate's voice wobbled. "I'm sorry. I haven't really told anybody that. I tried to tell…"

"Who?"

She hesitated, her voice hoarse. "My ex-fiancé, Derek. He looked at me as though I'd sprouted a second head." She cleared her throat. "But that's history. I'm sorry. I didn't mean to get off track."

"I wasn't crazy about the track we were on."

"Coming to the potluck that time was a good start. There's another one soon."

"Yeah…well…"

"I bet you used to do things as a family."

The memories were bittersweet. "Picnics, fishing, camping…"

"Have you done any of them since your wife passed away?"

"There's never any time."

"Can't your deputy fill in for you, so you can spend more time with Alyssa?"

If Owen did, then Tucker would have to face all

those things on his own. He couldn't imagine re-visiting them without Shelley.

Kate didn't push him, instead, letting the quiet linger, not speaking until the grandfather clock in the hall struck a quarter hour. "From what Alyssa says, your wife was a wonderful person. What do you think she'd want you to do?"

Move on. She'd told him in just those words before she died.

When he didn't reply, Kate glanced out the large kitchen window. "In Houston, my condo was on the eighth floor, but you know what? I can see more from here than I ever did there." She pointed to the squirrels that were squabbling by the big oak. "Those two argue about every acorn. I think I told you that, when I was a kid, we lived out in the suburbs—there it doesn't seem like the city, just houses on big lots. And we had squirrels, an occasional raccoon, more birds than you could count. After art school, I decided I wanted to be right in the city, close to the museums. Funny how distance changes how you feel about things."

He caught her meaning. But how could he let Shelley's memory drift away?

Move on.

"Fishing at the lake's pretty good," Tucker told her. "When the water's cooler, like it is now, you don't have to start out at five in the morning to catch something."

"Dad and I used to fish," Kate mused. "Haven't done it in years."

"Then I guess it's time to go again."

"That'll be great for you and Alyssa."

"Count yourself in."

About to take a sip of coffee, she stopped. "What?"

"Advice is only as good as it works. And you need to be on hand to see if it does."

On Saturday morning, Kate hurriedly finished gathering hats, sunblock and sunglasses. To her surprise, Tucker had organized a fishing outing that included Marvin. She thought it would be impossible to maneuver, but Tucker had arranged to borrow the church's van that was equipped with a wheelchair lift.

Marvin kept insisting it was too much trouble, but Tucker refused to take no for an answer. Kate offered to bring lunch, but Tucker had wisely refused that as well.

"Katie?" Marvin called out. "The van's here!" Excitement threaded through his voice and she smiled to herself. She hadn't told him that Daisy was coming along—that would make the day perfect for him.

She opened the front door just as Tucker was striding up the walk. Although he wore his usual jeans, he'd opted for a cotton shirt instead of his usual official sheriff's uniform shirt. This one allowed a peek at the top of his chest. Swallowing, she realized he managed to look even more masculine, just when she thought that aspect couldn't be pushed a smidgen further.

His dark eyes were brighter than she'd ever seen them. "Morning."

"Dad's probably going to beat you to the van," she babbled, trying to cover her reaction to Tucker.

"Then we'd better get going."

Marvin wheeled into the entry. "You sure this isn't going to be too much trouble? You kids can go on, so—"

Tucker walked behind the chair and grasped the handles. "Not getting out of it that easy. You don't want me outnumbered by the women, do you?"

Marvin chuckled, then visibly relaxed. It didn't take long for Tucker to get him out to the van where Alyssa waited. Kate slid in beside her, checking as she had every day for any signs of distress. Alyssa's eyes were clear. Still, Kate greeted her with a hug.

Tucker stepped in and took the wheel. "We've got one quick stop, then we're off to the lake."

They drove past only a few houses when he stopped, got out, and slid the side door open.

Daisy, dressed in casual clothes and a straw hat decorated with silk daisies, stepped up and inside.

The minute Marvin saw her, his face exploded in an ear-to-ear grin. "No one told me you were coming along!"

She looked anxious. "You don't mind then?"

"Ah, Daisy." The two words said it all.

She settled in and Tucker got behind the wheel again.

It only took a short time to drive to the lake. Kate hadn't been there before, and she felt like a tourist as she took in the towering pines that circled the deep, clear water, the wide banks, the quiet setting. Tucker drove to a spot beside the pier on the south side. Not far away was a picnic table and fire pit.

First, Tucker got Marvin situated on the pier, leaving Daisy with him. Then the other three pitched in to carry the fishing gear, along with a lawn chair for Daisy. So he wouldn't block access to the small pier, Tucker parked the van near a picnic table. There was another pier across the lake, and more tables scattered under the shade trees.

He was so capable. Realizing she was concentrating far too much on Tucker, Kate pulled her gaze from him, deliberately concentrating instead on the rest of their group. Her dad and Daisy were laughing and talking; Alyssa knelt on the wooden pier, opening the tackle box.

Kate walked halfway down the pier, stopping short of the others so she could watch her father and Daisy. Relaxed, Marvin was demonstrating baiting the hook for Daisy. She looked appropriately disgusted, then they both laughed. It was wonderful to see him so happy.

Tucker came up from behind, the solid ringing of his boots alerting her.

"Someone's having a good time."

She nodded. "Thank you."

Puzzled, he drew his brows together.

"For including my dad," she explained.

"He strikes me as the independent sort. Got to be hard on him, stuck in a wheelchair." He held up a lightweight pole. "This ought to be about right for you."

Since Marvin had his own tackle, he was all set. Tucker insisted he had extra equipment, bringing poles for Kate and Daisy.

Kate accepted the pole. "I don't remember much about casting."

He chuckled. "Good thing. We're fishing from a pier. If we were fly fishing we'd be on the bank, or in the water wearing waders."

She grimaced.

"Equals out. We only have to drop the pole in the water, but you've gotta use live bait, not a fly."

"Ick. I saw Dad showing Daisy, but I was hoping it was an option."

"It is," he agreed, a teasing glint in his eyes. "Either bait the hook or hop in the water and try to catch them bare-handed."

She gaped at him.

"It's a spring-fed lake," he teased. "Creates enough movement." He held up a small container filled with worms. "These wriggle well, too. Or we can use local bait—shad, nice and bloody."

She shuddered. "Oh, yuck! Can't I just use one of the plastic flies? They look pretty real."

"Even Alyssa baits her own hook."

Kate leaned over, taking a closer look at the worms. She sighed. "I could try the bare-handed thing."

He laughed, a hearty sound in the quiet. She'd never heard him laugh fully before. It surprised her so much she nearly forgot about the worms.

Tucker tapped her shoulder and the tingle it caused had nothing to do with bait. "Come on. I'll bait your hook, but that means you're more squeamish than a twelve-year-old."

She groaned. "I had to mention fishing."

"What? Aren't you bonding?" he asked with mock seriousness.

"Funny." She glanced over at her dad and Daisy. "Aren't they adorable?"

He shifted as he shook his head. "Not a word in my vocabulary."

Looking at over six feet of lean, muscled man, she couldn't disagree. Her throat suddenly dry, she tried to think of a quick change of subject. But her mind refused to move on…away from him.

"Come on." He shouldered a duffle bag. "Or we'll miss all the fish."

Her brow furrowed. Was he kidding? "Where would they go?"

"Even in cool weather, fish swim closer to the bottom when the sun's out."

"Oh. Like I said, it's been a long time since I've gone fishing."

He tried unsuccessfully to hide a grin.

She didn't blame him—he probably felt like laughing aloud. Then it dawned on her that the lake was more than just quiet, it was nearly silent, save the occasional splash of oars in the water, the nearly inaudible hum of voices. "I don't think I've ever been to a lake this quiet."

"No motorized craft allowed. Just canoes, kayaks—boats that are human-propelled. You can drive about forty miles to a bigger lake that allows all the noisy stuff. People respect this spot—don't bring radios or anything that'll make a racket."

"This has to be a rarity," she replied, impressed. "I'm surprised some developer hasn't tried to buy the property."

"Belongs to Rosewood. And we'll never vote to sell it."

"I hope not. People sometimes waver when it comes to money."

"Years ago, the town council held meetings to decide whether Rosewood ought to try to snare some of the tourist trade. But the town's a lot like this lake—unique. And the vote was overwhelming. Nobody wanted to give that up. The land outside the town's owned by people who've kept it in the family for generations." He shrugged, his face sobering, reflective. "But you're right, no one can guarantee the future."

Instinctively, she touched his arm. "We *can* make every day count with the ones we love. And that's what you're doing now. Look at Alyssa."

Tucker followed her gaze to the end of the pier. Together, they watched as Marvin teased her with an extra-long earthworm and both laughed.

"Yeah."

Although he didn't elaborate, Kate sensed the light flickering, if not fully dawning, on Tucker. She didn't expect this to be a quick process. She clutched her fishing pole. "Can I carry something else?"

"I've got it."

When they set up their poles at the end of the pier, Alyssa stood next to Kate, rather than her father. Stealing a glance at his expression, Kate could tell he was forcing himself to look unperturbed.

As promised, he took her fishing pole to bait the hook.

Feeling queasy, she tried not to show it. "I should do it myself."

"It's okay. One thing at a time."

She met his eyes, seeing that he had understood what she'd tried to convey concerning Alyssa.

Birds chirped overhead and ducks paddled toward the middle of the lake, occasionally diving beneath the water in search of breakfast. The quiet was enforced by the thicket of evergreens that forested the lake's shoreline. The sky, absent of clouds, reflected against the deep blue of the lake.

Although Kate tried to concentrate on fishing, she found herself studying Tucker more than the task at hand. He'd taken off his Stetson and his dark hair glinted in the sunlight. His profile...the strong jaw... But what she found more attractive was the man beneath the exterior. The one who wanted his daughter back, who wanted to make things right despite the grief he still battled.

Tucker glanced over at his daughter. She was still determined to distance herself, standing by Kate, interacting with the others instead of him. Maybe after today...

The lake was especially quiet, since so many Rosewood residents had gone to Fredericksburg for a music festival. Quiet enough for him to think. He'd been avoiding that as much as possible in the last few years. Probably why he'd spent so many extra hours on the job, keeping his mind occupied.

His gaze roved back toward Kate. He never would have guessed that anyone, especially a newcomer, could have persuaded him to turn his life upside down.

Alyssa's pole jerked. "Look, look!"

Startled, Kate pulled back. And Marvin couldn't maneuver his chair fast enough to help. Tucker leaned his own pole against the cooler and slipped in beside Alyssa. Caught up in the thrill of the catch, she didn't object as he helped steady the pole, then encouraged her as she battled the struggling fish. They worked together for several minutes before Alyssa could begin reeling the fish in.

Marvin passed a net to Daisy, who held it out, waiting for the first catch of the day.

Alyssa held her breath as the fish came into sight.

"Keep it steady, Lissy." Tucker directed her as the fish flopped on the end of the line.

"I am!"

Tucker took the net from Daisy and held it beneath the fish as Alyssa pulled it onto the pier.

"Wow," Kate murmured shakily, looking as though Alyssa had reeled in an electric eel instead of a catfish.

"It's a whopper!" Marvin declared, having turned his chair toward them.

"I'll say," Daisy added. She pushed back her straw hat. "Gonna be hard to beat this one!"

Looking squeamish, Kate smiled woefully. "I kind of forgot they flopped around."

"They rarely climb the line," Marvin teased.

Tucker removed the hook from the fish's mouth. Still working together, he and Alyssa put him on the stringer. "Good job, Lissy."

"It's not all that big," she dismissed, but a grin crept past her defenses.

"From the pier it is. Usually have to go out on a boat in one of the other lakes to get the big guys," Tucker replied. "But stripers fight like nothing else you'll find."

"Stripers?" Kate echoed.

"Striped bass. Not uncommon to get one thirty

pounds or more. The bigger lakes have white bass and catfish—blue and yellow."

Marvin's smile dimmed. "I hope I didn't keep you from going out in a boat."

Not wanting the older man to feel bad, Tucker waved away his concern. "Nope. I wanted to come here, but if we decide to go after stripers, I can get your chair on a boat. Pier fishing suits me. My dad used to bring me here when I was a kid." He glanced around their quiet, intimate setting. "And this is still my favorite spot."

"Grandpa Grey?" Alyssa asked in a small voice.

He put an arm around her shoulder, wishing his parents could have lived to know her. "Yep. He could coax a fish out of the water at the hottest time of day, middle of summer." Swallowing, he felt a renewed pang of loss. Despite coming to terms with their early passing, he missed his parents.

"Do you still go fishing with him?" Kate asked.

"He passed away," Tucker replied, not wanting to elaborate.

"I'm sorry. I—"

"Grandma and Grandpa Grey died before I was born, right after Dad graduated from high school," Alyssa explained.

Kate looked horrified. "I'm so sorry. I've heard

Alyssa talk about her grandparents—I just assumed…"

"It's okay." Tucker saw the genuine compassion in her eyes, the clear desire to empathize, to somehow make it better. Remembering she'd lost her mother at an early age, he knew it was sincere. "Okay, Lissy, let's put the string in the water, keep your fish cool. If we get any nibblers we'll bring him up, put him in the cooler."

Alyssa was quiet, but the banked anger that had simmered in her eyes since the autumn celebration was dimmer.

"Nothing like fried fish and hush puppies," Daisy mused. "I hope we catch enough for dinner."

"If Alyssa keeps going at this rate, we will." Tucker checked his own pole, then dropped the line back in the water.

"Dad won the local fishing contest five years in a row," Alyssa announced.

Surprised she had anything good to say about him, Tucker couldn't think of a reply.

Glancing up, he caught Kate's gaze, which was filled with obvious approval. She had discarded her hat, and her auburn hair shone like burnished bronze silk in the sunlight. He'd always been aware of the unique quality of her green eyes; now he noticed her delicate bone structure and how her lips naturally seemed to curve upward as though a smile was never far away. Being on the receiving end of that smile hadn't been a bad thing. Not bad at all.

Chapter Twelve

The swing on the front porch of the Lambert house was wide enough for two. Kate just hadn't imagined herself ever sitting in it with Tucker Grey. Especially as the moon rose in the dark skies otherwise illuminated only by emerging stars.

They'd caught enough fish for dinner; Marvin and Tucker cleaned them. Kate realized that Tucker suggested it so that her father could feel useful. And it worked. Tucker had piled newspapers on the kitchen table so Marvin could roll right up to the edge and dig in to the task. Combined with the fun of the day, he looked as he had before the accident—that all was well with the world.

Now he and Daisy, along with Alyssa, were playing dominos. Tucker had opted out of the game to check in with his chief deputy, Owen. And Kate wanted some air.

"You'd think I got enough air today," she remarked. "Maybe it's infectious…made me want more."

Tucker stretched out his long legs, crossing one boot over the other at his ankles, the thick heels thudding against the wooden planks. "Can't ever get too much of the outside. Seems like troubles aren't so bad."

Kate understood. Confined inside, thoughts tended to recirculate endlessly. "Is that why you decided to go into law? So you could spend time, at least some of it, outdoors?"

"No. Because of my parents." He paused. Time stretched out as he remained silent. Then he glanced toward the sky. "They were killed in a car accident because the other driver was drunk. I know I can't stop every accident, but I can make sure the streets of Rosewood and the highways in our jurisdiction are safe."

Kate swallowed, unable to imagine losing both parents at once. "I leaned on my dad after my mother died. Did…did you have anyone?"

"My sister got married a few months later, then moved to Iowa. I think she needed to get away. So it seemed like they hadn't died."

From what he left unsaid, she knew there hadn't been anybody for him. A few houses down the street, a dog barked. Late-season lightning bugs buzzed occasionally, like tiny, short-circuiting flickers. When she was a child, she thought they were actually filled with electricity.

Kate watched the insects. "I haven't seen fireflies in years. Makes me wonder if there aren't any left in Houston, or if I've just forgotten to look for them."

"Friend in Wyoming told me they don't have them out West—gets too cold."

"I'd have guessed most of your friends are here in Rosewood."

"Friend from college. Roomed together at A&M."

"You were still able to go to college…?"

"Had a football scholarship and I worked for the rest of what I needed."

She was impressed. Her father had paid for her education despite the high cost of art school. "I don't think I ever realized how lucky I was. How could I not know that?"

He chuckled, a humorless sound as quiet as the night. "How many people dwell on their good fortune?"

Although she knew he needed to move on for Alyssa, Kate felt the enormity of his losses. And she couldn't say something pat…no conventional words of comfort or empty promises. "Did you take art history in school?"

He nodded. "Thought I'd visit all the major museums some day."

"You still can," she reminded him gently. "It'd be a wonderful experience for Alyssa."

Pulling his legs back, he nudged the swing into motion. "We don't even get to Dallas these days."

Where Alyssa's maternal grandparents lived. She guessed Tucker must have met his late wife in college, too. But she was unwilling to go there, to pick at that wound. "I have a list a mile long of places I want to see," she mused.

"Places with great pieces of art?"

She held up her hands, using her fingers to tick off each destination. "Actually...I want to see the Liberace museum in Vegas, the Buddy Holly memorial in Muleshoe, the North Pole—you take a flight from Toronto and you just stay at the pole for a few hours, then fly back...um.... Iceland, the fjords in Norway, and Perth—it's on the far-west coast of Australia, the entire width of the country away from Sydney. Let's see..."

"No 'ten countries in ten days' kind of lady?"

Lady. Not a current term for women, which made it all that much more touching. Her grandmother had insisted she act like a lady. According to her, there were women and there were ladies. And Kate knew which category her grandmother thought she should aspire to.

He looked baffled. "What are you smiling at?"

"Nothing I can put in words." The gentle motion of the swing was in sync with her thoughts. Back and forth. Tucker was as complicated as he was handsome.

"I should round up Alyssa, get on home."

But he didn't move.

Enjoying the warmth of his lean, muscled body sitting next to hers, she didn't break the rhythm of the swing. "In the middle of a cutthroat game of dominos?" She shuddered in mock horror. "You're braver than I am."

He didn't make a move to leave. "How'd Marvin pick Rosewood to retire?"

"Dad and I used to take drives on Saturdays— just to see something different outside of Houston. We'd go to Hempstead, New Braunfels, Galveston, wherever the mood took us." She smiled at the memory. "Which meant, sometimes we wound up in pretty weird places. Anyway, when Dad retired, he started going on longer jaunts. He was looking for another town when he stumbled on Rosewood. After he'd eaten at the café, then stayed at the bed-and-breakfast, he said he was hooked. Liked the people, the area—everything. Before I knew it, he sold the house." Kate paused, remembering the renewed sense of loss when the house no longer belonged to her father. It had felt like she was losing her mother all over again.

"Wasn't easy giving up the family house." It wasn't a question.

And Kate realized he'd gone through the same thing. "What happened to your parents' home?"

"We sold it. Only seemed fair, so my sister could get her half." The memory reflected in his eyes wasn't a good one.

Orphaned. Five, fifteen, fifty—when your parents were gone, you became an orphan.

Kate let the soothing calm of the night and muted moonlight fill the void of words. When she'd met Tucker, she thought they came from different worlds. Strange how the distance was lessening.

He stretched his legs out again. "At least it's not a school night."

"Kind of. I have to finish getting my lesson ready for Sunday school. I did most of it yesterday. Just a few more finishing touches."

He was silent.

And Kate wondered what it would take to bring him back to the fold.

Tucker puttered around the kitchen the next morning after he walked Alyssa to church. She had asked him to stay, but he couldn't bring himself to go inside. Naturally, she was disappointed. And he felt he'd lost what little ground he'd regained on the fishing trip.

He sipped his coffee, but it tasted unusually bitter. Emptying the brew down the drain, he forcefully plunked the mug in the sink, just short of chipping it.

What had Kate suggested? Picnics…camping? From the look in Lissy's eyes that morning, she wouldn't be agreeable to another field trip anytime soon.

Because of church.

He looked out the kitchen window, up toward the clear sky. *"Why?"* he asked aloud. *"You got Mom and Dad. That wasn't enough. You took Shelley. Now you want Alyssa?"*

Instead of letting off anger, the words made his gut clench with fear. What if something happened to Lissy? He didn't want to lose her emotionally, but the thought of anything happening to her… It wasn't a new thought, but now it seemed more immediate, more possible.

He'd have sworn nothing could break their close bond. Rubbing his forehead, Tucker felt the onset of another headache. Didn't take rocket science to figure out why. Too much tension, not enough sleep.

Last night he'd expected to sleep better, after a

good day with Lissy. Instead, his mind had been filled with visions of Kate. He remembered her expressive face, how she'd shuddered in the face of baiting a hook, then, conversely, demonstrated the courage of her convictions. It was a quality he admired...except that it involved getting him back into the fellowship of faith.

He'd also dwelled on the sound of her laughter, how it blended so naturally with Alyssa's. And he couldn't escape the image of her delicate features, the curve of her smile, the lure of her eyes.

Or the fact that he hadn't wanted to end the day. Guilt nibbled, then took chomping bites of his conscience. He'd sworn there'd never be anyone other than Shelley. Never.

And yet... Kate's words popped into his thoughts frequently now. Both her warnings concerning Alyssa and her lighter conversations that could make him smile...think of her.

Tucker glanced at his watch. He had just enough time to head over to church and walk Lissy home. Out of habit, he'd dressed in his suit that morning to walk her there. His jacket hung over the back of a kitchen chair. Grabbing it, he stopped to check his tie in the hall mirror.

Timing it right, he arrived just before church let out. He waited at the edge of the circle of shade from the old oak, close to the sanctuary walkway.

When the deacons propped open the front doors, a surge of organ music preceded the pastor and congregation, emerging into the clear Sabbath day.

He responded to greetings as he watched for Alyssa. He knew his old friends and neighbors wondered why he hadn't joined the services, but no one questioned him. Instead, they offered warm words. His throat tightened. He had always been able to count on these people. They had offered support in the worst of times and had celebrated with him in the best. After Lissy was born, many had stepped forward, knowing his parents were gone. Just as they'd done when his parents had died. Like they'd tried to do when he'd lost Shelley. But his heart had hardened too much to allow them in.

Watching, he spotted Alyssa. She walked with Kate. Directly behind them, Daisy pushed Marvin's chair. The McAllisters scattered in and around the foursome. Emma walked on the other side of Kate, while Seth and Toby tried to ride herd on the twins. Seeing the toddlers, he couldn't help smiling. When Lissy was their age, she'd been a source of pure pleasure with her chubby little legs always pumping as she ran to discover any and every thing.

A few steps closer, Seth saw him and lifted a hand in greeting.

Seeing her husband's gesture, Emma rushed forward, hugging him. "Tucker! It's like I dreamed you up out of my thoughts!" She turned to Seth. "Right?"

"Yep. We're going to grill burgers, and Emma thinks we need to invite the whole town."

She elbowed him, then turned back to Seth. "If the whole town's five people. You'll come, won't you?"

His mouth was set to refuse, as was his habit now, but a glance at Kate and Lissy stopped him. "Is that what you want to do, Lissy?"

She nodded, her normal exuberance still dimmed.

He wanted badly to see it return. "Fine then."

A spark of hope returned to his daughter's expression. Looking over at Kate, he saw a matching flicker.

The McAllisters' backyard was large and friendly. Their dogs barked in greeting, remembering Tucker as though they'd just seen him a few days before, instead of two years ago. With the gate closed firmly, Everitt and Logan were allowed to roam, Toby making sure they didn't get into trouble. Alyssa helped him, clearly enjoying the energetic two-year-olds.

Kate helped Emma prepare the large table as the guys got the grill going.

"You'd think we were barbecuing prime rib instead of hamburgers." Emma filled a small dish with quartered lemons for the tea. "Guess it's a guy thing. To be honest, I can't tell the difference between the burgers we slap on the grill in a hurry and when Seth spends an hour prepping the fire."

"Thanks for having *all* of us, especially when you hadn't planned on it."

"These days, plans go right out the window." Emma straightened a placemat. "And I wouldn't have it any other way. I wish it weren't so cliché to say, but, seize the moment—because it's how I live now."

Kate was always cautious when a reference to Emma's murdered husband and daughter surfaced. She had become a valued friend and Kate didn't want to say anything that would cause her pain. "I've begun to embrace the same philosophy. A year ago, I couldn't have imagined Dad would be in a wheelchair. And I sure wasn't examining the rest of my life."

Emma's face filled with empathy. "You couldn't know what would happen. As for your ex-fiancé, it's *so* his loss."

"I was talking to Tucker last night—had an amazing epiphany."

"Tucker?" Emma questioned with upraised eyebrows.

Kate waved her hands dismissively. "Don't go reading anything into that."

"Why not?"

Kate scrunched her features in puzzlement. "You know exactly why. He deeply loved his wife."

"Who sadly passed away. But Tucker didn't."

Kate shook her head. "I'm just trying to help him reconnect with Alyssa."

"And you never noticed that he's a handsome, single guy?"

"I... I..."

Emma held up one hand. "Spare me. What you're doing for Alyssa is wonderful, and I think you'll be able to mend their rift. But that doesn't mean you can't go beyond neighborly help."

"You've forgotten. My record with men is abysmal. I dated Derek for three years before we got engaged, and even then it was a colossal mistake."

"Had you set a wedding date?"

"No."

"Which says a lot in itself. There isn't anything wrong with a long dating period, but it doesn't sound like an all-consuming love. The kind that says, yes, this is the guy I want to spend my life with."

Kate thought of Derek, how she'd admired his

drive, his accomplishments. But had there ever been that single, clarifying moment? The one Emma described? Though she resisted, Kate glanced across the yard, studying Tucker. Sure, she'd thought he was handsome from the day they'd met. And, yes, she admitted that she was drawn to many of his qualities. But he was still in love with his late wife.

Still… Swallowing, she felt a stir of emotion that swamped her thoughts, opened her heart. As she tried to sort out the unexpected tumult, Tucker looked up, catching her gaze. There was something in his eyes….

"Kate?"

Jerked from her reverie, she automatically placed her hand on Alyssa's shoulder. "Yes, Ally. Everything okay, sweetie?"

"Uh-huh. Toby said they're going to wear costumes at the library fundraiser!"

Absently, Kate smoothed back a stray wisp of Alyssa's hair. "What fundraiser?"

"It's for the school. To buy new books. So that's how come they're having it at the town library."

Her attention now fully devoted to the girl, Kate was delighted to see a flush of pleasure in Alyssa's face. "And what's this about costumes?"

"You can pick what you want to wear—from a book, or who wrote it."

"Sounds like fun."

"Will you go?" Alyssa beseeched.

Kate realized there was little she could deny this child. "Is it for everyone?"

"The whole town." She glanced over at Emma. "Toby said Miss Emma's making their family's costumes. Could we do that?"

"I'm not the best seamstress in the world, but I could try."

Emma didn't pause as she set out the silverware. "I'll help."

When Emma had been relocated to Rosewood, she'd left her legal career behind. Instead, she pursued her other passion—costume design. After marrying Seth, she'd sold the shop she'd established to her assistant. But she still liked to dabble in design.

"Wow." Kate looked at her friend. "Professional help? Won't you be too busy with your family's costumes?"

Emma laughed. "Soon as the event was planned, I started sketching. They're almost done."

"Do they have to coordinate?"

"No. The idea is to pick a favorite character or author and dress like them. So, unless your favorite is the same as who you're going with…" She grinned. "Some of ours aren't even vaguely similar."

"Who are you thinking of?" she asked Alyssa.

"I'm not sure."

"Wonder who your dad'll pick."

Alyssa's face sobered. "He'll probably have to work."

"Maybe not." Kate squeezed her hand. "Ally, you said you'd give him a chance. He would do anything in the world to make you happy. You know that, don't you?"

Reluctantly she nodded.

Kate knew that the strain of trying to be the adult in the family had gotten to Alyssa. That she'd protected, defended and even understood why her father had changed. But underneath she was still a child, one who missed her mother and needed her father to return to his parenting role. "He's trying." Speaking the thought aloud, Kate realized how difficult this was for him, yet he was determined to do the right thing.

Alyssa shifted uneasily. "I guess so."

Kate gestured subtly toward the tottering twins. "Sometimes, it's hard to see the steps, because they're small. And sometimes, people trip, but you can't let a stumble stop you."

Alyssa glanced down at her dress shoes, then smoothed her sides of her skirt. "Will you keep being my friend?"

"Oh, Ally." She hugged the girl. "That'll never

change. And you know something? I don't think your dad minds as much anymore." Kate lowered her voice. "And I think the reason he *did* mind was because he was trying to protect you, make sure you never got hurt."

"But the kids at school still talk about me. They say Dad's crazy."

Inwardly, Kate sighed, remembering the tortuous process of growing up. "They don't know him like you do."

When Alyssa didn't reply, Kate nudged her. "We need to be thinking about those costumes. Even with Emma's help, it's going to be a project. Okay?"

"Okay."

"You want to go help Toby with the twins?"

As Alyssa rejoined the kids, Emma finished with the silverware. "Good job."

Kate fiddled with the tablecloth. "You think?"

"You, my friend, are a natural." Emma handed her half of the stack of napkins and they both began folding them. "The girls in your Sunday school class think you're great, and Alyssa adores you."

"I've gotten pretty attached to her," Kate admitted, now certain she'd missed out by not having a family.

"Don't make it sound like a bad thing," Emma chided gently.

Kate tried to fold the napkin into a recognizable shape. Failing, she settled for a plain cylinder roll. "If Tucker ever moves on, which is highly doubtful, Alyssa could have a stepmother. She won't need her neighbor-slash-teacher."

"Tsk, tsk," Emma chided. "You may not be seeing Tucker in the right light, but from the looks I've caught, he's seeing you in a new one."

Unable to resist, Kate craned her head, staring across the yard. As she did, Tucker turned back to Seth. "He's probably just checking on Alyssa."

Kate felt her insides rattle. Emma must be imagining things, but she wished her words were true.

Chapter Thirteen

Feeling like a gorilla in a porcelain factory, Tucker cautiously lifted a delicate necklace from the window display. He had no clue if it was the sort of thing Alyssa would like. In his mind, she was still his little girl, more tomboy than teenager. But she loved all the things Kate bought for her. And he would be hopeless with clothes or barrettes.

Apparently, he was hopeless with jewelry as well.

He placed the necklace back, then looked up at a collection of bracelets. As he did, he glanced through the window, startled to see Kate on the other side.

Tentatively, she lifted a hand in greeting.

It was one of the few occasions when Rosewood was a tad too small.

She pushed open the wooden entry door. "Hey."

Feeling too large for the tiny boutique shop, he shifted awkwardly. "Do I look as foolish as I feel?"

Her smile was unexpectedly enchanting. "You look like a normal male. Jewelry stores aren't in your native habitat." She stepped closer, picking up a different sort of necklace. "This would look great on Alyssa."

So his intent was transparent. "Good thing I never have to work undercover."

She shrugged. "I don't know. You're pretty inscrutable."

"If that were true, you wouldn't be in here."

Her grin crept out again. "I'd be just as lost in a hardware store."

Amused, he studied the gold flecks in her eyes. "I think you just called me a Neanderthal."

"No. When I do that, you'll know."

He chuckled, unsure why she, only she, could make him smile. "Sandy, can you hold this necklace for me?"

"Sure, Tucker." The attractive woman took the piece. "The girls love these. Is it Alyssa's birthday?"

"Not for a while. Doing my reconnaissance."

"Sounds military," Kate mused.

"My dad was Army. Forward observer." He held open the door. "Thanks, Sandy."

The autumn air was crisp and newly fallen leaves nestled beneath the trees lining Main Street. It was just the kind of day he liked.

"Sandy's pretty," Kate commented.

"Suppose so."

Kate blinked, looking surprised. "Do you know her well?"

"Went to school with her." Along with everyone else his age in Rosewood.

"So...have you decided on your costume?"

Baffled, he stared at her.

"For the silent auction?" She stared back. "You don't have any idea what I'm talking about, do you?"

"Zero."

"It's a fundraiser to buy new books for the school, so it's being held at the library. Everyone comes as their favorite literary character or author."

He narrowed his eyes. "How'd you happen to find out about it?"

Kate licked her lips, then swallowed. "Well... from Alyssa."

And he hadn't heard a word.

"She thought you'd probably have to work," Kate hurried to explain.

"Um."

"She was disappointed to think you wouldn't be able to go."

He wasn't sure if that was supposed to be reassuring, or a shot at his inept parenting.

"Tucker, she'd be thrilled if you could manage to be there." Kate laid her hand on his arm. "She's hurting as much as you are. And she's confused." Her eyes searched his, an intense survey. "Have you talked to Donny Kimball and his parents?"

He didn't want to remember the humiliating incident. The Kimballs were understanding but also wary. Naturally, they were protective of their son.

"Her first crush." Kate's voice was soft. "It's a confusing time for a young girl. She's always had you to look up to. But then…"

He'd blown it.

"Anyway," she continued. "Donny's likely to be at the fundraiser—he's on the student council. I think it'd go a long way with Alyssa if you both attended. It'll reassure her that everything's going to return to normal."

"Which was a state you didn't think was very good."

She lifted her chin. "I don't know how I'd have handled your situation, so I'm not in a position to criticize."

His brow furrowed. Her attitude was a far cry from where it had begun. "Costumes?"

"It can be something simple. I told Alyssa I'd help with hers. And Emma offered to help, too."

He couldn't remember the last time he had to put together a costume.

"Think about it, won't you?" Her eyes were a clear green in the daylight. With her auburn hair, she looked like a beautiful Irish lass.

He tried to push the image away, since she continued to wait, entreaty etched in all her features. Realizing her hand still rested on his arm, he became even more aware of her soft touch.

"I suppose you have to get to work," she said finally, lifting her hand away.

He immediately missed the contact.

"And I need to finish up and go home," she continued.

"Is Marvin on his own?"

"Not often these days." Her smile turned conspiratorial. "He and Daisy have become quite good friends. She's over every day and he's really happy."

"Good women have that effect on men."

Kate raised her eyebrows, her mouth falling into an "O" of surprise.

The breeze lifted, ruffling her hair. *When had he last noticed a woman, as he was now?*

Kate shifted as she smoothed back her hair. "I'd better finish my errands."

"Yeah." As he watched, she walked away, disappearing into the drugstore. And it shocked him to realize how much he wanted to follow.

* * *

"Of course you should go!" Kate insisted, digging through a box of buttons. She held up a bottle cap. "Who organized this mess?"

Marvin shrugged. "I'm not even sure why I keep those. They never get matched up to the clothes." He paused. "I don't even know what a silent auction is. Once I went to a horse auction. Couple times I've been to car auctions."

"Silent auction's not much different. Instead of people calling out their bids, you write them down on a piece of paper. If you really want something, strategy is to make sure you write the highest price before the time ends. Just like a regular auction, you decide how much you're willing to pay. And, of course, all the money goes to charity—in this case, for the school. So, sometimes people pay a little more because they know it's for a good cause."

Marvin wheeled his chair backward. "Can't think of anything I'd want at the auction."

Kate threw out a bit of bait. "I happen to know that Daisy has her outfit planned."

Wheeling forward and pretending interest in a box of thread, Marvin pursed his lips. "What's she going as?"

"I'm not going to ruin the surprise." Kate picked up a purple button, wondering what it could be from. "Who's your favorite author?"

"Don't have just one."

"You love mysteries. How about picking a character from one?"

He shrugged, looking self-conscious. "My all time favorite's Perry Mason."

"Perfect. I only know him from TV reruns, but on those, he's almost always wearing a suit. Was it the same in the books?"

"Pretty much."

"Could be fun trying to get people to guess who you are."

"Maybe." He grinned suddenly. "Since Raymond Burr went on to play *Ironside* in a wheelchair…"

Kate remembered reruns of that TV show as well. "That's right! The policeman in a wheelchair. And, for Perry Mason, your character could have been in a boating accident, thus the wheelchair."

"Daisy likes mysteries, too," Marvin mused, trying to subtly coax her into revealing which character Daisy had chosen to dress as.

"I'm not going to tell you." Kate gave up on the button box. Thank heavens Emma was helping with her costume, Alyssa's, too. "That's up to Daisy."

He stared out the window. "Probably too much trouble to get me there in this chair. I can skip the thing."

A lump of emotion settled in her throat, but she

didn't give in to it. Even a man as tenacious as Marvin was susceptible to discouragement. "And miss what Daisy's wearing? I don't think so. I walk to Main Street all the time—this won't be any different."

Turning his chair around slowly, Marvin studied his daughter. "I can't help thinking how different your life is here. From the museum district in Houston to a tiny town in the Hill Country…"

"Dad, you couldn't have beaten me off with a stick. I'm where I want to be, doing what I want to do." She kissed the top of his head. "You know something? I was coasting in Houston. I didn't realize I was missing out on anything. Since I've been here…well…" It was hard to put in words. "You know I hadn't been to church in a long time. I forgot what a comfort my faith is. As for family…"

"This for *my* benefit?"

"Nope." She laced her fingers together. "I keep wondering how long I'd have stayed with Derek… why I never saw how he really is. I thought I knew exactly what I wanted—that I had it."

"I was blessed meeting your mother. Some people never find the right mate. Or a career they really love. Too many people marry the wrong person because they're scared to be alone. Just like they settle for a job that bores them because it's secure."

"You're still my rock, Dad."

"If we all go to this fundraiser thing, will you stop worrying about Derek?"

"Possible."

"You're good for me, Katie."

She tossed him a roll of pink print ribbon, which he caught easily. "Yeah."

He held up the ribbon. "Provided this doesn't have anything to do with my costume."

Laughing, she retrieved the ribbon. "You kidding? It's not even going on mine!"

Tucker inspected the shirt he'd just ironed. Didn't look too bad. He'd lived on his own enough to have mastered the basics. His mother had insisted that a boy needed to learn how to take care of himself just as much as his sister did.

He'd already brushed his felt dress Stetson. The weather had cooled enough that the straw hats were put away for the season. Before they'd fallen out, Alyssa would have popped in a dozen times to make sure he had everything lined up for his costume. She didn't sulk, didn't talk back. But the hurt and disappointment remained in her eyes. He would do anything to erase it.

His in-laws counseled patience. They had no

interest in seeing Alyssa separated from him. Though they mourned their daughter, they knew Alyssa belonged with him.

She had momentarily brightened when he told her he was going to the fundraiser. Then she'd questioned whether he was sure he would be home in time from work. She thought he wouldn't be. But, he'd taken Kate's advice. Owen Gibson, his chief deputy, was now in charge of the evening shift and he was scheduling weekend duty on a rotation basis. He'd also asked the state highway patrol for an extra cruiser during the busy weekend travel times. The process wasn't a snap change, though. He had to get it in place, and Alyssa didn't believe he'd follow through.

So, for tonight, he had tripled the manpower. Owen and two deputies were on duty. More than he needed, but he wasn't going to disappoint his daughter.

Alyssa had dithered back and forth about her costume, finally settling on a character from her favorite author, Louisa May Alcott. She'd read *Little Women* over and over again and liked the character Jo. Kate and Emma had worked on her costume. Kate admitted her skills were rudimentary, but Emma's were professional. Together they'd created a costume.

Once he was dressed, Tucker looked into the

mirror, hoping he'd picked something that wouldn't embarrass Alyssa. He straightened the string tie and felt the impulse to ask the Lord for help. His gut clenched.

"Dad?"

Trying to leave the feeling behind, he walked into the living room, stopping short when he saw Alyssa. Dressed in a post-Civil-War-era dress, she looked lovely. The full-skirted dress was light lavender, trimmed in ivory lace.

"Lissy, you look so grown up."

"So it's okay?" she asked anxiously.

"No." He squeezed her hand. "A whole planet better than okay."

She fidgeted, blushed, then finally met his eyes. "Really?"

He gestured over his chest. "Cross my heart."

Maybe he imagined it, but it sure looked as though some of her wariness was fading.

Tucker and Alyssa decided to walk over to the library. People from outlying ranches would drive into town, easily filling all the parking places on the street. And despite a faint nip in the air, the night smelled of late autumn, the moldering of damp leaves, the last traces of fading flowers. It was a smell not to be missed.

Alyssa didn't say a lot, but her nerves spilled into the quiet. "I wonder what everyone else will be wearing."

It seemed just a short while since she'd cared more about dolls than dresses, bicycles instead of barrettes. He'd been blind to the changes, but it didn't stop them from happening. "Won't be anyone there who looks better than you."

"You're *supposed* to say that."

"I'm supposed to tell you the truth," he corrected gently. "And it is."

"Dad?"

He slanted his head, listening.

"I think my friends will be there tonight."

Sighing inwardly, he hated that she feared he'd make another public display. "I know, Lissy."

As they approached the library, Tucker was surprised at the amount of cars that were parked by the library, spilling over into the nearby residential streets. From the sound of conversation and laughter, people were already gathering inside the large old building. The two-story stone structure had been built in the late eighteen hundreds. Both Texas pine and native limestone had been used inside for the walls and floors. Nooks had been created out of individual balconies on the upper floor, cozy places to curl up and get lost in a book.

The large main floor contained an ample communal space, along with rows of hardwood book shelves.

People in Rosewood loved opportunities to gather. While their little town didn't have what cities offered, the residents made up for it with social activities. Tonight's silent auction consisted of donated prizes, ranging from small craft items to a handcrafted armoire designed and built by Matt Whitaker, a local furniture maker. His pieces were famous all around the country.

Tucker was tentative as they entered, regretting that he'd cut so many people out of his life. Matt Whitaker had been his closest friend, but Tucker hadn't been able to let even him in. Because Matt counseled faith.

As Tucker walked further inside, people greeted him as though nothing had changed. *Forgiveness,* the inner voice intruded.

Alyssa looked around, presumably for her friends.

"Go ahead, Lissy."

She seemed nervous but excited as she darted into the crowd.

"Tucker!" Emma McAllister snagged his attention.

He turned, seeing that she wore a long gown and head covering that seemed to be from many centuries past. But his gaze stopped on Seth, who was dressed in a faux leather tunic that came to his knees and, of all things, green tights.

"I'm Robin Hood, okay?" Looking distinctly uncomfortable, Seth adjusted a quiver of arrows that was slung over his back.

Tucker did his best not to laugh. "Which makes Emma…"

"Maid Marion," she replied, dipping into a curtsy. Then she touched her head covering of silk, that matched her simple medieval gown. "It's called a wimple," she explained. "Fancy name for fabric hat."

"Well…" Tucker glanced again at his friend's tights. "It's sure authentic."

Seth grumbled under his breath.

"So, what's Toby? One of the Merry Men?"

"Superman," Seth replied. "He's not into medieval."

"You look great," Emma told her husband, adjusting the cowl at his neck.

Seth caught Tucker's amused gaze. "Yeah."

"She's right. Downright merry," Tucker added, grinning when Seth held back what he really wanted to say, since his wife stood at his side.

Seth grumped off and Emma followed him.

"What's their hurry?"

Hearing Kate, Tucker spun around. For a moment it felt like he was still spinning when he looked at her. Her long burgundy gown brought out the beauty of her eyes, the richness of her flowing hair, accentuated by a crown of flowers. The flowing dress, with its fancy puffed sleeves, looked as though it was made of silk and some heavier fabric he couldn't identify.

"Tucker?"

He tried to clear his head, which was difficult since Kate still stood in front of him. "Um. Seth's bent out of shape because Emma's got him in tights."

"I think their costumes are great." She let her gaze roam from his crisp western shirt to his usual jeans and boots. "So…you are your favorite character?" she teased.

"Louis L'Amour's my favorite author. You probably don't know his work."

"I've always admired the lyric, poetic quality of his writing," she replied. "I was crushed when I finished his last book and found out it was one of the few published after he died."

He was surprised. Being in the library reminded him, even if was cliché, not to judge a book by its cover. He studied her beautiful burgundy gown. "And you?"

"I always loved the musical, *Camelot*, that was based on T.H. White's book."

"So you're Guinevere?"

She shook her head. "I've never thought of myself as a queen." She bowed in a partial curtsy. "Just a lady of the court."

Funny, he'd been thinking she looked like a Celtic princess. A beautiful, enchanting dame of the highlands.

She laughed quietly. "Probably no one here will even get it. The *Camelot* thing, I mean. Or know anything about it."

He met her eyes, those unique, enchanting green eyes. "Don't let it be forgot, that once there was a spot, for one brief shining moment, that was known as Camelot."

She seemed mesmerized as he took her hand and dropped a quick kiss on her soft skin.

"How did you know that?" she asked, her voice low, husky, her hand trembling in his.

Her hand was silk, he decided, a surreal extension of her exquisite gown. "It may be legend…" He shrugged. "Or a noble bit of the past."

"Noble," she echoed.

He still held her hand and she suddenly wished he would never let go.

Chapter Fourteen

As Tucker wove through the crowd toward the punch bowl, Kate stared. *Noble.* A word that described him perfectly. Upholding the law because it made the world a better place, raising his daughter on his own. Was there anything nobler?

Unable to stop watching, she saw that he looked even more handsome than usual with his western-cut leather jacket and highly polished boots. He was so different than any man she'd ever known.

And she felt more for him than any other as well. How had this happened? She knew it couldn't go any further, that his heart was already taken. And she couldn't hope to compete with a love so deep, so rich.

Looking up, she spotted Alyssa with Donny Kimball. Tucker was only a few feet away and she hoped he could keep it together. Over the last several days, she'd reassured Alyssa that it would be different tonight, that Tucker wouldn't over-react.

Seeing that Tucker went one way, the kids another, Kate pivoted, noticing the variety of outfits people had chosen. She couldn't help smiling at her dad and Daisy, who had been circulating since they arrived.

Marvin's eyes had lit up when he saw how classy Daisy looked dressed in a 1940s suit, with its flattering jacket and pencil skirt with a kick pleat. True to the time period, she wore an elegant hat that gave her an air of mystery. And pinned to her lapel was her trademark gold brooch, fashioned in the shape of a daisy.

Marvin looked handsome in his best suit, with a new, jaunty red tie. She waved, and they maneuvered in her direction, reaching her just as Tucker returned with the punch.

He handed Kate one of the cups and offered the other to Daisy. "How 'bout you, Marvin? Can I get you something to drink?"

"In a bit." Marvin studied Tucker. "I know you're either a western character or author. Zane Grey?"

"Close. Louis L'Amour. And you're….?"

Marvin straightened his tie. "Not easy to guess."

Tucker scratched his head. "I could guess about a dozen authors. Want to give me a hint?"

"Actor who played him went on to star in *Ironside*."

"Ah, Perry Mason."

Marvin chuckled. "I'd about decided anyone under fifty hasn't heard of him." He pointed to his leg. "I'm Perry Mason *after* a boating accident."

"Sounds reasonable."

Marvin gestured to Daisy. "Want to guess who she is?"

"Author or character?"

"Author," Daisy obliged, a twinkle in her blue eyes.

"From the forties," Tucker mused.

Kate was surprised he could recognize the decade.

As though reading her thoughts, he grinned. "I like to watch old movies. Lissy and I have a system—three new movies to every one of my old ones. Works 'cause the percentage of new movies pretty much drowns the old." Narrowing his eyes, he studied Daisy's outfit. "Wild guess— Agatha Christie."

"That's right!" Daisy exclaimed. "How did you know?"

"You've always been a mystery fan. And Ms. Christie *is* the best-selling author of all time."

Kate stared at him. Tucker was revealing layers she hadn't guessed existed. Sobered, she realized she'd pegged him and put him in a box. And he was spilling out of that box, crumbling its sides, flattening her uninspired expectations.

"The town theater group's thinking of putting on *Mousetrap*," Daisy confided, referring to the world's longest-running play, based on Agatha Christie's book.

"Are you going to try out?" Tucker asked.

Daisy demurred. "I don't think so."

"Why not?" Marvin drew his eyebrows together. "You'd be great."

She blushed, her fair skin blooming with a flattering pinkish glow. "I don't know."

Kate guessed this was a discussion that would continue.

"I'll get some more punch," Tucker offered.

"You having a good time, Katie?" Her father asked as Tucker dove back into the growing crowd.

"Perfect. I love costume parties. Hats off to whoever thought of this, instead of a boring chicken dinner or something like that."

"It was Emma's idea." Daisy patted her own hat, making sure it was still slanted just right. "She's the one who encouraged me to pull out the trunk with my mother's things. After Mom passed away, I picked some of her favorite things and stored them."

"I'm sure she'd be very pleased," Kate murmured, noticing her father taking Daisy's hand in his. "Emma never even let on that this was her inspiration." Glancing away, she didn't see Tucker, but she was pleased to see Alyssa and Donny approaching.

Although Kate had seen her costume in different stages as it was made, she hadn't seen Alyssa in the finished dress. Kate felt so proud, she wanted to bring the girl to everyone's attention. Instead, she quietly told her dad and Daisy, who both beamed as they caught sight of her.

"She's growing up so fast," Daisy bemoaned. "I can remember when she was a toddler."

"Tucker's got to be proud of her," Marvin added.

Kate digested this thought. It hadn't occurred to her that Tucker might be proud of some of the changes in his daughter. Shortsighted of her.

"Ah, Miss Alcott, I believe?" Marvin greeted her.

"Yes, kind sir." Alyssa bowed slightly, the lavender ribbons on her hat trailing. Emma had fashioned the bergère—a shallow-brimmed hat of ivory straw.

"I thought you were going to come as Jo," Kate

questioned, referring to the main character in *Little Women*.

"I was." Alyssa fidgeted. "But Dad decided to come as an author...."

Kate blinked back an unexpected sting of emotion. Having prayed that Tucker and Alyssa could repair the hole in their relationship, it thrilled her that they were on the right road.

"And Miss Emma said the costume could be for either Jo or Louisa May Alcott." She pinched one side of her long skirt. "Do you think so?"

Tucker arrived with the punch. "I do. And I've read *Little Women*—it was part of the curriculum when I was your age." He handed Marvin one cup of punch, then held up the other. "Alyssa? Donny?"

Kate held her breath, praying this moment would go well.

"We just had some punch, sir," Donny replied nervously, in his changing voice, going from tenor to alto to a near soprano.

Tucker nodded. "Then this one's mine." He looked around at the others. "So Alyssa told you about her costume?"

A chorus of affirmative answers garbled out.

Unperturbed, at least on the surface, Tucker sipped some of his punch. "Did you get a look at Matt Whitaker's armoire? I've heard there are out-of-towners here to bid on it. He's got a year-long waiting list for his work. No wonder there's so much traffic."

Alyssa's bright expression dimmed. "Does that mean you have to go on patrol?"

"I tripled the deputy shift tonight. Owen's in charge. He can handle whatever comes up."

Stunned, Alyssa didn't reply.

So Kate did. "What a clever idea. That way you could be sure to be here."

"Especially since you didn't have advance notice about the extra visitors," Daisy commented. "But for once, I don't mind the tourists. If they're bidding, Matt's piece will bring in even more money. Probably some dealers in the crowd."

"I wondered why we saw so many trailers," Kate exclaimed. "I didn't think there were that many large items in tonight's auction."

"Lot more hopeful buyers than big pieces," Tucker replied.

Marvin carefully balanced his cup of punch. "Katie's painting ought to bring a good bit."

Tucker looked surprised. "You have something in the auction?"

Kate wished her father hadn't mentioned her painting. "Just something I dabbled with."

"But you said you weren't an artist." Alyssa glanced up at her.

"I'm not."

"She is, too," Marvin retorted.

Having second thoughts about donating the painting, Kate glanced around their small group. "Technically, I've been trained as a painter, then a restorer. But it's a stretch to call my painting *art*. Emma bent my arm to donate it."

"Don't listen to that," Marvin insisted. "She's good. At both things—painting and restoring. This one's a copy of the painting she made for me back in art school."

"And you're so unbiased," Kate replied, embarrassed that the group's attention was riveted on her.

"Wait till you see her painting," Marvin insisted.

Kate gave in. "Thanks, Dad."

"I guess we'd better go see what Amber and Sasha are doing." Alyssa spoke to her dad. "We said we'd be right back."

"Have a good time." Tucker then met Donny's nervous gaze. "You, too, son."

Kate knew how difficult it was for him…these baby steps that were taking Alyssa to an age when she would no longer be his little girl.

After they left, Tucker leaned close, lowering his voice. "Do you know who Donny's supposed to be?"

Since the boy appeared to have used several rolls of tin foil in his costume, it was hard to say. "Sci-fi, I guess, but I can't tell who. I'm pretty sure it's not the tin man from *The Wizard of Oz*."

Tucker grinned. "At least he's not wearing green tights."

"Is Seth still grumbling about that?"

"You blame him?" Marvin commiserated.

Daisy shook her head as she grasped the handles of the wheelchair. "Men."

Kate chuckled as the two set off to look at more of the auction items. "Emma spent hours on their costumes."

Tucker's brow furrowed. "Can't imagine why. Seth feels like a girl in those tights."

"A man's worst fear?"

His expression changed in such a way that Kate caught her breath. When he didn't reply, she felt compelled to fill the pocket of silence between them. "Do you know why Alyssa chose to be Louisa May Alcott instead of one of her characters?" Kate paused, still sensing the charged feeling between them. When he didn't reply immediately, she hurried the rest of her words. "Because she knew you were coming as an author, so she wanted to as well."

"You sure?"

"Positive. You're taking steps to keep your promise. And she sees that."

"Have you looked at everything that's being auctioned?"

She took the change of subject in stride, knowing he didn't like talking about his feelings. "Not all of it. You?"

"Nope."

The auction items were positioned on tables that had been cleared of their displays. Given the age of the library and much of its contents, the tables varied in size and shape. For the fundraiser, most had been moved to the front area, but a few that couldn't fit were still lodged between the stacks.

Kate didn't particularly want to see if anyone had bid on her painting. How embarrassing would it be if no one did? She stared at the composition: father and child walking on a wide roadway. For a moment she wavered, thinking it might be less humiliating to bid on it herself. Almost as quickly, she chucked the notion, deciding desperation wouldn't be any better.

Moving along, Kate found a wood carving she thought her dad would like, and added her bid to the clipboard. Then she bid on a pair of embroidered guest towels Daisy made. And she bought half a dozen bars of chocolate from the kids.

Stowing them in her purse, she resolved to give away all but one. Well, maybe two.

Although there was interest in all the donations, people crowded around the clipboard for Matt's piece. Looked good for the book fund.

The winning bids would be announced at the end of the evening. For a while, Kate mingled with the people she knew, realizing that number had grown. Despite not wanting their town to be a tourist spot, they welcomed newcomers in a way she hadn't known existed.

As the crowd grew in the library, Kate decided to step outside for some air. The brocade material of her gown was thick. It had seemed a bit too warm inside, but the air outside was cooler than she'd thought and she shivered.

"Cold?"

She spun toward the sound of Tucker's deep voice. "I didn't know you were out here."

"Little crowded in there for me."

"Me, too."

"Not used to crowds anymore?"

"I never liked crowds, but there are lots of good things in the city, too." Feeling chill bumps, she rubbed her arms.

Tucker slipped off his jacket and draped it over her shoulders. "Doesn't really go with your dress...."

He stood close enough for her to smell the clean scent of his soap, a whiff of subtle aftershave. Also close enough that she could watch how his dark eyes changed in the moonlight.

Kate didn't mind that he'd stopped talking. Her own words dried up.

The breeze played with the leaves scattered across the sidewalk, ruffling those still attached to their branches. And the cloak of evening muted any distant sounds, making them all but fade away.

Kate felt the amplified proximity to Tucker.

"You look really nice tonight," he finally murmured.

She couldn't come up with a fast quip, even a lame one. "Thanks."

He touched her silky sleeve. "Like you stepped out of the pages...."

Kate swallowed, feeling her heart race. He was wounded, she reminded herself. And still in love with his late wife. But her heartbeat didn't slow.

Moonbeams cast pewter puddles in the shadows. And the thrumming against her ribcage escalated. Hesitantly, she raised her gaze, and saw that his eyes were tortured. His visible pain pierced her heart.

The silence, heavy and dense, draped around them like a fog. And Kate wasn't sure if the fog would lift, or herald a storm.

"Dad! Kate! It's time to find out about the silent auction! Who won and stuff…" Alyssa added, with a question in her last words.

"Great." His voice was hoarse.

Kate wondered if her own would remain steady. "Can't wait to see."

Awkwardly, she and Tucker walked inside, keeping Alyssa between them.

"Did you bid on anything, Kate?" Alyssa was all but jumping up and down.

"A few things." Still shaking inside, Kate tried to focus on the auction, the people, anything but the glimpse of Tucker's pain, the feelings he evoked, the trembling of her heart.

"I've been saving my allowance," Alyssa confided.

As they found seats not too far from the front, Kate concentrated on everything except Tucker.

Emma stood at the podium, the head librarian beside her. Seth was nowhere in sight, apparently hiding his colorful tights.

"First of all, we want to thank everyone for coming out tonight and for all your support," Emma began. "New books for the school is a great cause."

Polite applause scattered, then died away.

Emma grinned. "Now, on to what you want to hear. We're going to announce the successful bidders of the most expensive items first. We've tagged some of the smaller items with the winners' names, so feel free to circulate while I'm speaking."

The librarian handed Emma a paper.

"We want to thank Matt Whitaker for donating this valuable and exquisite mahogany armoire. The successful bidder is Brandon Ellis of San Antonio." A mix of disappointment and approval roared through the library. "Congratulations, Mr. Ellis. Can we ask if this is going to your gallery or your private collection?"

The sleek, dark-haired man stood. "Haven't decided yet. You all come visit the gallery." He winked. "Best way to find out."

Laughter cut through the groans.

Emma announced the next few items: an antique spinet piano, a guided fishing and camping weekend, a set of nineteenth century porcelain cups.

Kate tried to act normal, as though there weren't tears lurking just beneath the surface, that she didn't have feelings for a man who could never return them.

A round of applause followed the announcement of each successful bidder.

"I should probably go check the pieces I bid on," she managed to whisper, starting to rise.

Alyssa tugged her back down. "Wait. The thing I want ought to come up real soon."

Kate was so unsettled she'd neglected to ask what Alyssa had bid on.

Then Emma held up an antique locket. "The successful bidder is…"

Alyssa leaned forward in anticipation.

"Tucker Grey."

Confused, Alyssa looked at her father. He patted her knee. "Thought you'd look great in it."

"But I bid on it, too!"

"I wanted to get it for you. That okay?"

Watching Alyssa hug Tucker, Kate accidentally met his gaze over her head.

Alyssa pulled away. "Did you see it, Kate? It's way cool!"

"I'm sure it is, sweetie."

"I'm gonna go look at it again." Alyssa popped up as soon as the words were out.

Kate was conscious of the sudden empty space beside her…next to Tucker. Clearing her throat, she clutched at conversation. "How'd you know she wanted that necklace?"

"Easy. I watched and saw what she bid on. And I knew her allowance wasn't going to be anywhere close to the winning bid."

"That was sweet."

He lifted his eyebrows. "I don't get that often."

No. He wouldn't. People saw him as the strong, steadfast sheriff. Not a man who loved deeply, forever. Looking away, she saw that Emma was holding up her painting. "Someone bid," she blurted out.

"You didn't think anyone would?"

Kate shook her head.

"Hmm."

"We had quite the bidding battle over this piece," Emma announced. "Painted by Rosewood's Kate Lambert, *Yesterday,* goes to…Tucker Grey. Congratulations, Tucker!"

Gaping at him, Kate was so confused she thought her head might burst.

"You want to know why I bid on it."

She nodded.

"I like the subject, the composition…the artist."

Her throat was a Sahara of dryness.

"You ought to paint more." Tucker twirled his hat in front of his knees. "The last of the wild-flowers will be gone soon. They'd make a good backdrop—you ought to sketch them."

She still couldn't believe he'd been the one to bid on her painting.

"Did you get what you wanted?" he asked.

"What?"

"You said you bid on a few things."

"Oh. Right." She tried to collect her thoughts.

"I should probably go see if they're tagged." Rising, she slipped between the metal folding chairs.

He followed. "Think you got the wood sculpture for your dad?"

"What'd you do? Video everything?" Including her thoughts? "How'd you know it's for my dad?"

"You don't look like the buffalo sculpture type. And, with my job, you have to notice everything."

Great. Had he noticed her heart nearly beating out of her chest?

Kate kept walking until they reached the western wood sculpture. She'd bid high, then bid again when someone had outbid her. Her name was on the tag as the successful bidder.

"What else did you bid on?"

"Just some guest towels." She looked around, trying to remember where they were. Tucker continued following as she searched for the towels. When she found them, she chuckled.

"You win again?"

"No. My dad outbid me."

"A gift."

"I doubt it. Daisy made them. I'm thinking he wants to make sure I don't take them when I leave."

"Leave?" Shock laced his voice.

"When my dad's recovered," she explained.

"I thought you moved here."

"In the sense that I sold my condo in Houston and put my furniture in storage. But Dad knows the plan wasn't forever."

His lips thinned and the pain returned to his eyes. "I nearly forgot. It's never a good idea to count on forever."

Chapter Fifteen

"Kate tells me you bought her painting." Marvin wheeled to face Tucker while Daisy poured the coffee and Alyssa munched on a fresh doughnut.

He nodded. "I told her she ought to sketch the last wildflowers. Won't be long now till they're all gone."

Daisy handed Tucker a steaming mug. "That's a great idea!"

"Yeah," Alyssa reaffirmed between bites. "We could do that today."

Tucker hadn't structured the Saturday morning, deciding to let it flow naturally. That seemed best these days, but he hadn't planned an outing that included Kate. He sipped the hot brew, wishing he hadn't mentioned the wildflowers.

Kate brought in the pair of warm trousers

she'd mended for Alyssa. "I don't think the tear shows, since it was on a seam. If it doesn't hold, we can ask Emma—"

"We're going to take you to draw flowers!" Alyssa announced, waving the last of her doughnut. "If you want, I mean."

Confused, Kate glanced at the others. "I must have missed something between here and the bedroom."

"Tucker told us about you wanting to sketch the last of the wildflowers," Marvin explained. "Great idea."

She was trying not to look surprised, Tucker noted. Not all that successfully. They'd kept their distance since the night of the fundraiser. And she didn't look too crazy about going any-where with him.

And that suited him fine. For the briefest moment, he'd let Kate crack the shell he'd erected around himself. But he'd been yanked back down to earth when she casually mentioned she wasn't staying. He knew he was being irrational, but the feeling was out of his control.

And that's what bothered him.

He'd pledged his heart, his life to Shelley. How could he have even a stirring of emotion for Kate? Much less, the deeper feelings that were rooting in his heart?

"I'm sure you must have more fun things to do," she demurred.

"Uh-uh," Alyssa reassured her. "We didn't plan anything."

Except bugging him to bring over her trousers to be repaired. He'd added a run to the bakery for doughnuts, so they wouldn't seem to be there only to ask a favor.

"Um..." Kate looked around. "Did I put my mug down in here?"

"It's on the counter," Daisy replied, pointing to the box from the bakery. "And doughnuts so fresh they melt in your mouth."

"Ally, I told you you're killing my willpower," Kate teased.

"It wasn't my idea. It was Dad's."

Her fingers already touching a doughnut, Kate hesitated before lifting it out. Her gaze darted up, barely meeting his, before she returned her attention to the pastry. "Very thoughtful."

"I think I'll have to eat another one," Marvin announced. "Not often you get them when they're still warm."

Kate put another doughnut on a paper napkin and carried it over to her father.

"Dive into yours," he advised, accepting the treat. "Don't wait till it gets cold."

Tucker watched as Kate took her first bite. No longer in the muted evening light, no longer wearing a fairy-tale dress, she shouldn't look as appealing. To his chagrin, she looked even better.

Alyssa brushed her hands together, dislodging bits of glaze. "What's wrong, Dad?"

Realizing he was frowning, Tucker tried to hide what he was thinking. "Just thinking we need to get a start on the day."

"We *are* started," she replied, looking at him quizzically.

Trust her to have that reminder ready. "Marvin, you feel like getting out?"

"Too much hassle getting the church van."

"Besides, he has a date for Scrabble," Daisy added with a twinkle.

"Then maybe we should wait for another day…." Kate began.

"Dad knows all the best places for the flowers," Alyssa piped up. "When he was little, his mother showed him all the fields where they grow. And they come back every year, always."

"A forever thing," Kate murmured.

Tucker did his best not to give in to the gut reaction the word caused.

Because he wasn't sure she really understood its meaning.

* * *

Kate clasped and unclasped the pad and pencil in her hands. The backseat of Tucker's SUV had been folded down to accommodate archery equipment, a picnic hamper, soccer ball and lawn chairs. Her art tote was stuck in there, too. Not wanting to disappoint Alyssa, Kate had fallen in with her plans.

Kate got in the vehicle. Before she could blink, Tucker took his place behind the wheel and Alyssa slid in the passenger side, trapping Kate in the middle. Not wanting to make a fuss about sitting next to Tucker, Kate pressed her arms to her sides, trying to make herself as narrow as possible.

"There's lots of room," Alyssa assured her, fishing for the seat belt buckle.

Great.

As they drove toward the outskirts of town, other drivers waved as they recognized Tucker. It was a small town thing, Kate supposed. A friendly sort of thing.

"The bluebonnets bloom in the spring," Alyssa informed her. "We get lots of tourists on the highway then."

Kate was having a hard time keeping her thoughts straight as she sat pressed against Tucker's side. "Probably good for the bed and breakfast."

"Keeps it busy." Tucker turned onto a dirt road.

"Between birdwatchers and flower followers, most of the Hill Country's full of tourists."

"Flower followers?"

"Season's nearly year-round, when you include all the wildflowers. The *flowerphiles* go where the blooms are."

"We go, too," Alyssa added. "Well, not so much lately, but we used to go when our favorites first bloomed."

The ruts in the dirt road deepened, bouncing them around. Every time a bump knocked her against Tucker, Kate automatically stiffened. Even so, she felt the rock-hard muscles of his arm.

Tucker slowed down, then parked on the side of the road. He pointed through the windshield at a patch of white. "Up there."

Alyssa scrambled out of the SUV first. Within moments, they were hiking through the field of wild grasses. As they got closer, Kate could see that the solitary flowers grew on slender individual stalks rather than in clumps. Low and bushy, they grew in mounds a foot tall and twice that width. The reedy stalks each held a bloom, broad white petals that surrounded a small, yellow, central disk.

"I'm not sure what they are, but I'd guess white zinnias," Kate ventured.

"Lots of folks think that," Tucker acknowledged. "They're blackfoot daisies, native to Texas."

She sniffed the pungent air. "They smell like honey."

"In the spring, the butterflies are all over them because of the scent." Alyssa waved her arms around as though she stood in her own personal field.

"That must be something."

"Next spring you can come up here and see the butterflies." Spotting a jackrabbit, Alyssa strayed away.

Saved from replying, Kate bent to touch the petals. "I wonder how they grow without any care. They must really be hardy."

"About six years ago we had a long drought— lasted a few years, but they just kept on growing."

"Amazing how strong the Lord's creations are." She glanced up, expecting to see a mask of anger. To her surprise, his face was filled with loss.

"I'll get the stool and your art stuff," Tucker offered, turning back to the car before she could comment.

Holding her sketch pad, she spun slowly, looking in every direction. The flowers appealed to her, but she wanted something else, something more. Just then, Alyssa popped up from the ridge of the hill.

Kate sat on the ground and began sketching, capturing the essence of the gently sloping hill, the tree-lined ridge, the yellowing wild grass that fluttered like young stalks of wheat.

The blackfoot daisies remained in the background, poignant remains of an ending season. But the forefront of her sketch was dominated by the charm and enchantment of Alyssa, her bright young face, the unqualified beauty of a child becoming a teen.

"You need any of this?" Tucker held out her stool and tote.

"I might use the stool in a while, but I'm good with just my pencil."

"How will you remember the colors?"

She shrugged. "I can come back and take a few photos."

He disappeared and Kate set to her task, not wanting to lose Alyssa's spontaneity.

Back at the car, Tucker took his digital camera from his glove compartment, where he kept it to photograph accident scenes. He took a few wide shots from the bottom of the hill, then climbed deeper up into the field, pausing to look through the lens. Alyssa popped through the trees, much like a butterfly herself. He lowered the camera, pausing when he lit on Kate, then focused. Her pencil still, she was watching Alyssa. But his focus was on Kate's face.

Sunlight accentuated her pale skin, classical profile…her full lips as she smiled. The graceful arch of her neck was more pronounced, since she'd pulled her hair back in a loose ponytail.

Kate's interaction with Alyssa was so natural, unforced. Since he'd never considered another woman entering their family dynamic, it floored him to see Alyssa's acceptance of Kate…her seeming need of the relationship.

He ignored his own need.

At least he tried to.

After roughly penciling Alyssa's figure, Kate added Tucker to her sketch, trying to capture his strength, his unique personality, his dark good looks. As she finished up, she thought of the upcoming spring, whether she would be in Rosewood. Or if her father would be well enough for her to return to her life. Despite having reexamined her choices a lot lately, she still didn't know what she was going to do.

Tucker approached as she applied the last strokes to her drawing. She quickly jerked the cover down, but he had already seen the sketch. "I have enough for today." To her surprise, something unexpected, something unrelated to her sketch, flickered in his eyes.

An inexplicable ether thickened the air, brought them both pause. Birdsong and the breeze carrying it seemed to mute. Kate wondered if she imagined the change...that, and the beat of her heart tripping, climbing.

She still sat on the ground. Tucker held out his hand. Accepting it, a connection from her heart to her body ignited. Shaky, she stood, not releasing his hand immediately. Was it a shared sensation? His eyes had darkened, his hand remained in hers. She swayed inches closer.

"Can we shoot now?" Alyssa shouted.

Tucker and Kate jumped apart as though Alyssa had actually shot them.

"Shoot?" Kate asked shakily, reaching up to smooth non-existent flaws in her hair.

"Archery." His voice was husky, almost raw.

Running, Alyssa skidded to a stop between them. "Ready?"

Kate tried to sound normal. "Is there a range close by?"

"Range?" Alyssa questioned.

"We use the trees," Tucker explained. "We hang a target so the bark's not damaged."

"Oh." Feeling very much the fledgling she was,

Kate trailed them down the hill to the SUV, where they unloaded the equipment.

Tucker pointed to a copse of trees opposite the field. "This'll do fine."

After trudging across the road, they stopped before they reached the trees.

Tucker laid his bow and quiver down, holding only the target. "I'll hang this."

"Won't you need a hammer and nail?"

"We've shot out here before. We try to keep the number of nails to a minimum." He easily found a nail on the tree and positioned the target.

Alyssa immediately picked up an arrow and positioned the nock. "Okay?"

Safety measure, Kate supposed.

"Since Kate's our guest, why don't you let her have the first shot."

Kate waved her hands in dismissal. "No! Let Ally go first. I actually haven't held a bow since high school."

Tucker nodded and Alyssa let her arrow fly, hitting a good mark.

"Do you remember how to hold the bow?" he asked.

"Not really."

He demonstrated the stance. "Put your bow in position."

Kate tried, but she was all thumbs and then some.

Tucker lowered his own bow, set it aside and walked behind her. He stretched his long arms around hers, placing her hands in the proper position. Her mind befuddled by his touch, she couldn't concentrate.

"Think you've got it?"

Kate cleared her throat. "I suppose. There isn't anything behind the trees I might hit, is there?"

"Deer have already caught our scent and jack-rabbits are too close to the ground. Bobcats and coyotes usually stay higher in the hills."

It was all Kate could do not to squeeze her eyes shut before she took her first shot. The arrow struck the tree, just not the one with the target.

"That's okay," Alyssa assured her. "First time I didn't even hit a tree. Had to look all over for the arrow."

Touched by the child's seamless, never-failing compassion, Kate hugged her. "You're good for me, you know that?" Then she held up her bow. "I remember actually liking archery in school."

"You're just rusty." Tucked plucked an arrow from his quiver. His shot flew steady and sure, piercing the bullseye.

Kate rolled her eyes. "What are you? An Olympic archer?"

Alyssa giggled.

Tucker's lips pursed as he tried not to laugh. "We're not standing all that far from the target."

"High school obviously was longer ago than I remember," she admitted, with a grin of her own.

"Doesn't look like it."

Despite her best efforts, Kate blushed.

"Can I shoot?" Alyssa asked.

"Sure, Pop-tart. Then we'll get Kate set up again."

It took numerous tries, but Kate finally hit the right tree. Not the target, but at least the right tree.

"You don't want to shoot too much the first time," Tucker advised after about an hour. "Your shoulder and arm will really feel it."

"I'm okay," she assured him, not wanting to cut into this time Tucker and Alyssa were spending together. Also not wanting to end it for herself.

But a little while later, Alyssa laid her bow down. "Can we have lunch now?"

"If you ladies are ready."

"Ready!" Her arm throbbing, Kate realized she'd spoken a little too fast, as Tucker's face eased into a smile. And it hit her. He smiled more now, more naturally.

They'd brought along a quilt to spread on the ground. Lunch was simple, but good. Alyssa lifted the last container out of the hamper. "Surprise! Brownies."

Kate groaned.

Tucker's brow furrowed. "You don't like them?"

"Alyssa knows I can eat a plowman's share of her brownies."

Tucker looked at Alyssa, then Kate. "So, what's the problem?"

Kate wished she hadn't said anything. "I don't need to eat them."

"Women," Tucker muttered, reaching for a brownie.

Biting her lip to keep from laughing, Kate took a brownie. "We *are* a mystery, I suppose."

Tucker sighed heartily.

And Kate laughed aloud, her self-conscious-ness disappearing. This was fun, just hanging out with him.

Stuffed with brownies, they were loath to move. Alyssa tugged on their hands as she flopped back on the quilt, pulling them down on each side of her.

"I see…" Tucker mused.

"An owl with a hat!" Alyssa said as she stared at the cloud formations.

Kate could remember watching clouds with her mother all those years ago. She'd said that clouds were like dreams, and every life needed dreams.

"What do you see, Dad?"

"Um…clouds?"

Alyssa giggled. "Really."

"A horse. He's galloping. Almost gone."

They all stared at the sky. A cushiony wealth of clouds drifted across the warm, blue expanse. Perfect for cloud watching, since the shapes changed at just the right pace. For a moment, Kate thought she could see her mother's face, a glimpse of her smile.

Tucker lifted his head, speaking across Alyssa. "What do you see, Kate?"

"Dreams," she murmured. "Just dreams."

Chapter Sixteen

Tucker printed the last of the photos from their day. Although Alyssa had gone to bed hours earlier, he hadn't been able to sleep. Too much on his mind. Television didn't distract him; he only got through a few pages of the paperwork he'd brought home. He didn't have as much left over lately. He'd delegated some of it, and he could get his own done more quickly.

But the camera called out to him. Normally, he edited the photos, printing only the ones he handpicked. This time, he felt compelled to print all the shots.

He flipped through the first several—views of the field, close-ups of the flowers that he'd taken, to document their colors. Then he'd shot some frames of Alyssa. Ah…she was growing up too fast.

His hand stilled. Kate smiled up at him from the

page. Unguarded, her eyes were filled with something close to glory. As natural as the grasses and flowers surrounding her, she looked like a wood nymph rising from the earth.

Without conscious intent, he traced the outline of her smile, remembered its warmth.

Carefully, as though handling fragile glass, he picked up the next photo. And the next. When he came to one with both Kate and Alyssa he stopped. Alyssa knelt next to Kate, and although they didn't share the same physical characteristics, somehow their smiles matched.

A lump formed in his throat. As some of his anger faded, Shelley's image was beginning to blur. How could that be?

His hand rested on the photo, picking it up along with one of only Kate. How had he never noticed the impish upturn of her nose when she teased Alyssa? Or the twinkle in her eyes that even a camera could capture?

Instantly, he was reminded of her compassion, her kindness…her faith. He tilted back in his old wooden chair, comforted by its familiar creaking. Memories of turning to the Lord washed over him. It was a comfort never matched by anything else. Emptiness resided in his heart where his faith once was. His father's words resounded in his thoughts: "Turn everything over to Him and the Lord will always guide you, always be there for you."

Tucker rubbed one hand over his forehead, feeling a twinge of pain. It occurred to him that he hadn't had a migraine in quite some time. Not since…

Sighing, he closed his eyes, longing for the assurance he'd once received from the Lord. But he couldn't let it go, couldn't forgive. The ache in his heart came from more sources than he wanted to admit. More than he could reconcile.

A few days later, Kate stood at her easel, working on a tiny patch of the painting. Although her father claimed that her supplies weren't at all in the way, she had her doubts. Whenever possible, she gathered up her paints, brushes and bottles of restoration chemicals when she finished up for the day. But sometimes, when she was in a hurry, she had to leave them, returning to a messy living room. In Houston it didn't matter so much; distances in the megacity necessitated making arrangements before driving to a friend's. But in Rosewood, neighbors and friends casually dropped by, and she hated them to see the mess.

Sometimes, she thought of setting up some sort of studio in the garage, maybe putting in a larger window. She still didn't know how long her father would need her. And she'd fiddled around with the idea of staying in Rosewood even after he recovered. Of course, then she could get her own place.

But that made her think of Tucker and Alyssa, wondering how difficult it would be to live close by and not be part of their lives. In time, Alyssa would want to spend most of her free hours with her friends. And Tucker… eventually he'd find someone. Pain rippled through her at the thought. Without warning, silent tears rolled down her cheeks.

The doorbell rang, loud and sharp.

Feeling ridiculous, she swiped at the tears, then yanked open the door.

And stared at Tucker.

He took off his hat. "You have a minute?"

"Sure." Her voice was hoarse, almost gravelly. She led him into the living room. "Um…." She cleared her throat. "Have a seat."

"Looks like I'm interrupting your work."

Her face still averted from him, she waved her hand in dismissal. "I haven't really gotten into it today."

He leaned forward. "You okay?"

Rubbing her forehead with one hand to hide her eyes, she faced him. "Sure."

"Have you been crying?" Concern threaded his voice as he stood.

"Of course not."

"Then why are your eyes all red?" he demanded.

"What are you, the eye police?" Immediately realizing the absurd irony of the question, she sighed.

He didn't laugh at the slip of words. "What's wrong?"

She searched desperately for a reasonable explanation. "I was just thinking that if I stay here, I'm going to need more room. I'll have to set up the right kind of table—I can't always work a restoration on the easel."

His expression changed, his eyes darkening, questioning. "Is that what you're planning?"

Kate wished the floor would open and swallow her whole. This was the last thing she'd intended to discuss with him. "I...I don't know."

"Is there someone back in Houston who'll affect your decision?"

For a minute, she thought he meant her friends. "Derek? No. Haven't reconsidered that."

"Then what is it?" Stretched to his full height, he towered over her.

Instinctively, Kate took a step back. "It's not that simple. Is everything always so black and white for you?" Knowing she wasn't making sense, she wanted to end the conversation, remove his disturbing presence. "Was there some special reason you came by?"

He stared at her hard, finally pulling out an envelope from the inner pocket of his jacket. "I took photos of the field and flowers, so you'd have the colors right."

The simple but touching gesture unnerved her. "You did?" Her hand fluttered to her chest.

"Wait too long and the flowers will be gone for the season."

"Oh."

He handed her the envelope. "There's a pretty good one of you and Alyssa."

Surprised, she opened the packet, flipping through the photos until she saw one of herself and Alyssa. Tucker had captured a perfect, priceless moment. Suddenly breathless, she slumped down on the couch which was directly behind her.

Immediately he sat beside her. "What?"

Holding the picture, her hands trembled, but she didn't speak.

Tucker allowed the silence to linger.

Kate tried to pull herself together. "I have a picture kind of like this one—of my mother and me. I was younger, but…" She blinked back the threat of tears. "It's sad and good all at the same time, you know? But, this one… It makes me wonder if I'll ever be the adult, the mother, in the picture."

"Because you broke up with Derek?"

The pain she'd felt earlier multiplied. "No."

"I'm not any good at guessing."

Keeping the tears back was excruciating, but she was determined not to give in to them. "How do you know I'd admit it if you guessed right?"

His brow furrowed. "I feel like I stepped inside a puzzle with half the pieces missing."

"Half?" The irony screamed at her. "Maybe you're not so bad at guessing after all."

He was clearly baffled.

She glanced down at the pictures. "Thanks. For taking these, I mean."

"Kate." His voice was slow, deliberate. "You've done a lot for Alyssa—well, for both of us. We'll help you…anything you need."

Her middle name should be irony. How about falling in love with me? Getting past your grief to even see me?

She interlaced her fingers to keep them steady. "Yeah."

Tucker looked as though he wanted to say more. Instead, he awkwardly patted his hat against one leg before rising. "Better leave you to it then."

Again biting her lip, she nodded as she, too, stood.

He tried to catch her gaze, but she shifted, walking toward the door. "Say hi to Alyssa for me."

"Kate?"

She clutched the doorknob.

He put his hat on, then hesitated. "Bye now."

"Bye." She watched his strong profile as he walked away. And wished he didn't have to.

Unable to sleep, Kate wandered into the living room. She'd eaten a quiet supper with her father and Daisy, insisting on cleaning up so they could talk. Daisy had become such a permanent fixture in the Lambert household, Kate couldn't picture a day without her in it. Although she respected her father's dedication to her mother's memory, she wondered if he'd ever allow someone to share his life. Much like Tucker.

Not that he would change. She deeply respected Tucker's loyalty, the depth of his love for his late wife. It wasn't a love that could be duplicated. Because, with his heart already full, there wasn't room for her.

She lifted the cloth covering her easel. Unable to forget her reaction to Tucker the afternoon they scouted wildflowers, she'd begun a new painting, one with both Tucker and Alyssa in it. In the back of her mind, she knew she wanted something to remember them by when they were no longer part of her life.

Needing a distraction, she checked her e-mail. She weeded through the messages, pausing when she came to one from the Houston Museum of Fine Arts. They had a job for her—one that needed to be done on site, because the canvas was so large. The department head, knowing Kate's situation, added that the starting date was flexible.

Leaving Rosewood. And Tucker.

Kate stared at the screen until the message blurred. Save or delete? Reluctantly, she pushed Save. Uninterested in reading any more of her mail, she signed off.

Trailing into the kitchen, Kate flipped the light on over the sink. She filled the teakettle and set it on the stove. She could hear her grandmother's advice—that a cup of tea always helped. She chose an herbal blend from the pantry. Once the water boiled, she dropped the tea bag in the cup. And listened to the silence.

During the day, there was always the hum of some sort of noise—voices, television, kitchen clatter. But at one in the morning, it was so quiet she could be the only person on the planet. And that was a lonely place to be.

Stop feeling sorry for yourself! Her father had

always told her that, when she was down, she should thank the Lord for all her blessings. After reciting all the good, the bad didn't seem so dismal in comparison. In fact, the problem often seemed too petty to include in her prayer.

As Kate recited her blessings, she realized they were many and great. All of her father's follow-up visits had been positive. He was healing as the doctors had hoped. Alyssa was a blessing who would always remain in her heart. Kate's horizons had been broadened, at the same time grounding her in a way she'd never been before.

Ending her prayer, she lifted the tea bag, swirling the liquid. The cup had just reached her lips when the kitchen screen door banged. Startled, she dropped the cup, shattering the china, splashing hot tea on herself and the floor.

Was it windy outside? She listened intently, but couldn't hear the normal sounds of a storm. No branches brushing the windows, no clatter of the metal vents on the roof. She didn't want to investigate, but… *You're being ridiculous.* There were any number of explanations for the noise, but she couldn't think of a single one.

She dug in the odds and ends drawer and found a flashlight that worked. Drawing her shoulders back, she eased open the back door. The light bobbled around the yard, but she couldn't see anything. Reaching back, she flipped on the porch light. Frozen, she stared around the partially lit side of the house. No hulking intruder leapt out at her, so she finally breathed.

Still, she was eager to get back inside and lock the door behind her. She did, then leaned against the wood and glass door, tickled by the curtain that fluttered across the glass portion.

The fear eased. Expelling her still-uneven breath, she took one step. And a sudden scratching, grating noise turned her movement into a leap. Immediately, she thought of her father. They would be helpless against an intruder.

She grabbed the portable phone and crouched down beside the counter. Without hesitation she punched in Tucker's mobile number. He answered before the second ring.

"Kate?"

"Tucker," she whispered. "We need help."

"Stay on the line," he ordered. In the background, she heard the quick thrust of his boots hitting the floor. Evidently he was still up. "Do you need an ambulance?"

"No." Her voice was barely audible, but the fright apparently came through. "I think someone's trying to get in."

"Front or back?"

"Back, by the kitchen door."

"Where are you?"

"Kitchen."

"Stay out of sight."

She scooted as far back as she could, stopped by the wall.

"Where's your dad?"

"His room."

"Get in there with him and lock the bedroom door."

"But—"

"Do it!"

Kate complied, crawling from her hiding space into the hall, then running to her father's room. Her dad, oblivious to the drama, snored lightly. Thankfully, the wooden blinds were closed, so no one could see inside. Frantically, she looked around the room for something to barricade the door. But anything that would keep someone out was too heavy for her to lift or drag on her own. And what if they needed to get out in a hurry? Compromising, she slumped against the door, blocking it with her own weight.

Minutes passed and her fear escalated. What if Tucker had been taken down by the intruder? He could be wounded, passed out, bleeding.

"Kate?" Tucker's quiet voice penetrated the door.

Startled, she flipped back, knocking her head on the wood floor.

"Kate?" he repeated.

Reaching up, she unlocked the door. He pushed it open, saw her sprawled on the ground and knelt to help her up.

"Are you hurt?"

"No, I… Who was it?" She didn't let go of his hand as he led her to the kitchen.

"*What* was it would be a better question."

"'What'?" she asked numbly, not understanding.

He tugged her toward the back door.

"Are you sure…?"

"Come on."

Still hanging on to him, she reluctantly stepped outside.

"Over here."

Cautiously looking around in a circle, she allowed him to lead the way to a bushy area at the side of the house.

He pulled back the boxwood and azaleas, exposing an uneven wooden cover on the ground.

"What's that?"

"Used to be a larder," he explained, lifting off the dilapidated cover.

"Oh my!" A smallish brown dog, hovering over what looked like a new litter of pups, stared back. Kate knelt down. "You poor little thing, out here in the cold with your babies." Her fear forgotten, she looked up at Tucker. "How do we get them inside where it's warm?"

In the muted backyard light, his face softened. "You want to take on raising them?"

"They can't stay out here! The mother was probably trying to find food."

"Or getting the space ready. The wood on the cover was crumbly enough for her to squeeze by to get down inside." He knelt down beside Kate. "We'll need a good size basket or box, clean newspapers, towels."

"I can do that." She put her hand out, palm side up, for the dog to sniff. Passing the sniff test, she then stroked the dog's ears. "Everybody needs some help now and then. You don't have to do this alone."

Tucker was quiet.

"I wonder if she's just lost," Kate murmured.

"No tags," he confirmed, "or collar. I'll check with the county animal shelter. No local reports of missing dogs at my office—we always follow up on those as soon as they come in. And the vet can scan her, see if she's got an ID chip."

"Seems like somebody who'd pay for a microchip would also have her spayed." Kate continued to stroke the dog's long, silky ears. "Well, little mother, we're going to get your transport ready and you'll be all warm before you know it."

* * *

Having called Owen to cancel backup help, Tucker found a box that was the right size, while Kate collected the rest of what he needed. Daisy spotted the lights and activity from her house and offered to stay with Alyssa until he was done. Although his daughter was safe enough, he never wanted her to be alone in the night.

The little brown dog didn't resist their help. To the contrary, she seemed relieved to be taken inside with her pups. Working together, Tucker and Kate set up a quiet out-of-the-way spot in the laundry room, just off the kitchen. Although Marvin woke up when he heard the noise, he was content to see the new additions in the morning. Noodle, however, leapt to the counter, then vaulted to the top of the refrigerator. Perched there, he suspiciously watched the small strangers.

"Do you think we should have the vet check her out?"Kate asked, looking worried.

"Wouldn't hurt. He can scan her then."

Kate adjusted one of the towels. He noticed that she didn't hesitate to use her plush designer linens for the dogs. "I'll have to get some food in the morning. I wonder if she needs extra vitamins?"

Tucker felt another small part of his heart thaw. She was fussing like they were human babies. "Once the light's out, she'll probably go to sleep."

"I'll just leave a small lamp on in the other room. But I'd better stay with her, make sure everything's okay."

"You're going to sit on the hard floor all night?"

"Bet you've done about the same. With Alyssa, I mean. You can't sleep when you're worried about little ones."

So he had. Kate had so many instincts of a natural mother, he had to remind himself she didn't have a child of her own. Her head bent close to listen to the pups, the reminder faded. But not the feeling it created.

Chapter Seventeen

Alyssa was over first thing the next morning. Since it was a school day, she'd quietly tapped on the kitchen door in the early hours of dawn.

"They're so tiny," she whispered, immediately falling in love with the three little pups.

"I know," Kate whispered back. "Of course, their mom's little, too."

"What are you going to name them?"

"For now I'm just calling them Snap, Crackle and Pop."

Alyssa giggled. "But they don't make any noise."

"Your dad assured me they will, in time. I'm going to have to get a book on what to do, what they'll need. That, and ask the vet."

"I wish I could stay home from school today and help."

"Trust me, you'll be drafted after school."

Alyssa sighed. "Dad told me not to stay long. He's such a grinch."

"You know he found them?" Kate questioned gently. "Actually, he rescued them. Otherwise they'd still be out in the cold, maybe not make it."

"He didn't tell me that." Alyssa's eyes rounded. "I just thought…"

"You know he doesn't brag on himself," Kate reminded her. "He saves all that for you."

"Really?"

Kate nudged her. "You know he does."

"I guess."

"Any more notions to live with your grandparents?"

"Nah." Alyssa chewed on her bottom lip. "I just wanted everything to be normal, like my friends. Guess that can't happen."

"If it could, your dad would wrangle the moon and the stars to get what you want. But life changes when you lose someone you love." She paused. "Especially someone as important as your mother."

Alyssa stared at the pups.

"You know your dad's doing his best?"

Alyssa blinked several times, then a single tear escaped.

"Oh, sweetheart!" Kate threw her arm over Alyssa's shoulders. "What's wrong?"

"I was pretty mean to him…." Alyssa gulped. "And…"

Kate hugged her close. "He understands."

"How do you know?"

"Because your heart is part of his." She rocked Alyssa in a gentle motion. "And that will never change. Never."

The morning light gradually brightened, spilling through the windows, shining on the most fragile, illuminating the most blessed.

Tucker double-checked his records, confirming there were no local reports of missing dogs. He had explained the situation to Owen, so they would be on alert for any new reports. Then he called the vet, Zeke Harrison, explaining the situation.

Zeke agreed to pay a house call to the new mother. One of the advantages of a small town. Zeke's house calls were usually restricted to large animals, but he didn't mind making an exception. It wasn't the first time the compassionate veterinarian had gone out of his way for his patients.

Alyssa had called on her lunch break, pleading to go home early. Knowing she'd feel the same the next day and the one after that, he had to say no. But he'd tried to soften the refusal by telling her that Kate would need more of her help in the evenings. He'd expected her to go silent. Instead, she asked if they could go to the pet store and buy the dog a collar. He'd agreed, cautioning her that the dog might have to be returned soon to its owner.

Thinking of Alyssa now, it seemed his daughter had her old lilt back in her voice. Shifting mental gears, Kate popped into his mind.

His phone rang, distracting him. His irritation faded when he heard Kate's voice, inquiring about the vet.

"He said he can stop by this evening." Tucker pushed back the old chair. "That work?"

"Yes! Oh, Tucker, she is the best little mother you've ever seen! Daisy used to always have a dog until her last one died about a year ago. Anyway, she bought the right food this morning and poor little Dotey ate like it had been a month since she'd had a real meal."

"Dotey?"

As Kate laughed, he heard a trace of self-consciousness. "Because she dotes on her puppies. You can laugh now."

He smiled to himself. "I can let that one go."

"Alyssa called between classes to check on them," Kate confided. "It was so sweet, Tucker."

As was the feeling he got from listening to Kate's voice.

"Tucker?"

Reluctantly, he returned to business. "I told her you'd need more help in the evenings." He remembered Alyssa's changed tone. "She didn't argue about it."

Kate didn't answer immediately, and he could picture her holding the phone, absently twirling a lock of hair. "Good."

A gratified note in her voice made him wonder if she had something to do with the change in Alyssa.

"Maybe you'll be off work soon enough to be here when the vet comes." Kate paused. "If you want, I mean."

The warmth grew. "See what I can do."

By day's end, the county shelter confirmed they didn't have reports of any dogs even vaguely resembling Dotey. They sent an e-mail of reported lost dogs, complete with pictures: a poodle, black Labrador, border collie and a schnauzer. The only mixed breeds were one boxer-lab mix and one Dalmatian-Lab mix. Neither resembled Dotey.

Zeke was at the Lambert house when Tucker arrived. Entering quietly through the back door, nobody noticed him. They were all crowded around Dotey and her pups.

"Yea!" Alyssa shrilled. Then she clapped her hands.

"So it's positive?" Kate was asking. "No chip?"

Zeke put the portable scanner back into his bag. "Nope. I don't recognize her either. And I'm the only vet for a lot of miles. Unless Tucker's found out something different from the county, I'd say she's a stray."

Tucker thought of the irresponsible pet owners who drove to the country to dump off unwanted dogs and cats, usually dealing them a death sentence. Ones that weren't hit by the highway traffic often starved, lost and alone. It was a miracle this dog had made it to the Lambert house. *Miracle.* His thoughts tumbled. Once he'd never questioned miracles…ones from the Lord. But…

"Dad!" Alyssa burst out of the laundry room. "Kate said I can have one of the puppies!"

"Whoa." Kate emerged right behind her. "I said you could *ask* your dad about a puppy."

"They're *so* cute!" Alyssa continued, pouring all of her convincing ability into the three words.

"I have seen them," he replied dryly.

"Kate said you rescued them. If it hadn't been for you, they might not even be alive."

His eyes darted to Kate's.

Her expression was steady, supportive. "It's true."

"Maybe the Lord knocked on the back door to help the process along," Marvin added.

Before Tucker could reply, Zeke engulfed his hand in a hearty shake. "Been too long, Tuck. Don't wait for another stray." They had been friends since childhood, going to both school and church together.

"Thanks for doing this."

"Thought I was going to have to get arrested to see you," Zeke joked. "Hope I see you at church soon."

Swallowing, Tucker glanced around the circle of expectant faces. And couldn't speak.

Kate stepped forward. "Thank you again, Zeke. I feel so much better knowing Dotey and the pups are okay. And it was great that you could take the test samples right here. I don't think she wants to be separated from her babies."

"No problem. I'll let you know the results tomorrow." He thumped Tucker's shoulder. "Really good to see you."

Zeke left to a chorus of farewells. Weighed down by his thoughts, Tucker didn't join in.

"Zeke said he thinks she's probably a Tibetan-spaniel mix," Kate told him, obviously trying to smooth over the moment. "Once Dotey can have a bath, I think she'll look a little more golden. Her fur's long and it's pretty matted." Kate shoved her hands in her pockets, a telling sign of her anxiety.

"And she doesn't belong to anybody!" Alyssa celebrated.

"You'll need to wait a little while to be sure," Tucker cautioned. "Shouldn't take too long. I'll e-mail authorities in the surrounding area. If she's been reported missing, we'll know in…say a week or so." It was easier to talk about the dog, anything except his faith or feelings.

Alyssa wasn't deterred even a fraction. "Dr. Zeke put little tags on the puppies so we can keep track of them for the tests and stuff. Maybe we can get them all matching collars."

"They won't need collars for a while," Kate assured her. "I don't think Dotey's going to wander far from her puppies."

But he had wandered, Tucker realized. From everything that had once rooted his life. Still… The unhealed wound in his heart told him he hadn't sought this path; it was the one he'd been dealt.

Kate checked on the puppies. They were a week old and utterly adorable. Dr. Harrison had prescribed some routine newborn meds. And Dotey had gotten some necessary injections. It had been an intriguing week, filled with the joy of three tiny new lives.

And the loneliness of not seeing Tucker once in

the same time. Although Alyssa had been a near-constant presence, Tucker had stayed away. Going over her actions the last night she'd seen him, Kate couldn't figure out what she'd said or done wrong.

Giving Dotey one last pat, Kate stood, wandering over to the kitchen window. Staring up into the sky, she didn't see any answers, only the graying of several clouds. She'd gotten out of the habit of checking the daily weather. Unlike Houston, it didn't rain as often in the Hill Country, although they did get a thorough drenching now and then.

She swallowed, thinking of Tucker, remembering how readily he'd come to help her when she'd thought there was an intruder. But that was his job, she rationalized. He never once indicated there was anything more between them than their shared concern over Alyssa. Kate threw her head back, trying to remember. Had she somehow shown her feelings? Was Tucker staying away because of it?

"Penny for your thoughts," Marvin said, rolling to a stop.

"Not sure they're worth that much." Reluctantly, she turned to face him.

He immediately looked concerned. "Katie Bear?"

"I'm just being silly, Dad. Nothing to worry about."

"Not one of your traits. What's going on?"

She fiddled with a spoon on the counter. "Just wondering why Tucker hasn't come around. It's been a week."

"Work could be heavy."

"Alyssa's been going home on time every day, so I don't think so." She put the spoon back down. "I don't know why I even mentioned it."

"Katie, have you ever been able to fool me about your feelings?"

Eyes down, she shook her head.

"He's a good man. You couldn't have fallen for a better one."

"Fallen?" She mustered up an objection. "I—"

"Why don't you want to admit it?"

She slumped back against the counter. "Pretty stupid, huh? I've known from day one how much he loved his wife, how losing her has crippled him. How he can't ever love again…."

"Katie, Katie…" He rolled closer. "You're just going to give up like that?"

Tears pushed past her resolve. "I can't compete with the ghost of such an enormous love."

"The way he loved his wife proves he can love you just as much."

"But—"

"He has enough room in his heart for you, Katie.

Remember, I've been there. I know exactly how he feels."

Kate didn't want to hurt him, but she had to ask. "Then why didn't you ever remarry?"

"It has to be the right person—whether you're thirty or sixty." Marvin glanced up and out the window toward Daisy's house. "And then you have to act on it."

Kate bent to kiss the top of her father's head. "Thanks, Dad."

He patted her arm, then looked out the window again.

She wondered at the look on his face. "Think it might rain?"

He pulled his gaze from Daisy's house. "Looks like we're in for a real gully washer."

"Really? I have to get some drops for the puppies. And the vet's outside of town."

"You don't want to get caught in bad weather. Storms can come up fast here." He wheeled back toward her. "Can't it wait?"

"Be better if I have the drops today. Besides, you know I've been driving in rainstorms since I got my license. Houston's not exactly known for its dry weather. And it shouldn't take long."

But it was better than an hour later when Kate left the house. The phone didn't stop ringing, including her client who wanted an update on the restoration. And that put her in mind of what she had to tell the Houston museum. She still hadn't replied to their e-mail.

The clouds continued to darken as she drove out to Dr. Harrison's. His practice was on a small ranch with ample space for the large animals he treated. With all the cattle and horses in the area, he stayed busy. But Daisy had told her the doctor had a real soft spot for dogs and cats.

Dr. Harrison wasn't in, but his assistant, a vet tech, checked Dotey's file, then brought out the drops. When the tech asked about them, Kate couldn't resist telling the woman all about Dotey and her pups.

By the time Kate stepped back outside, the wind had picked up, buffeting the remaining leaves on the trees. And the clouds were gathering, darkening even more. She hadn't meant to stay so long. Looked like her father was right, a storm was brewing. She hopped in the car, shivering at the quick drop in temperature. She was glad to be inside. Good thing her little car was snug.

She'd only gone a few hundred feet when the rain began. Not soft-landing, big drops. But hard, fast, driving rain. Flipping her windshield wipers on high, Kate also adjusted the defroster. Yipes.

Her dad wasn't kidding when he said storms came up fast. But the rain didn't worry her. Houston had as much rainfall as a rain forest, often filling the streets to over capacity, flooding many of them. She'd literally been in deep water more times than she could count.

Still, she wished she'd gotten an earlier start. With the sun obliterated, it was so cloudy that the day looked much like evening, gray and obscure. Kate watched carefully, since she didn't know this road. Any low spots could fill with water. Driving slowly, she was relieved not to see any pockets of deep water that could drown out the engine.

Someone honked behind her, wanting her to speed up. *Idiot*. She wasn't driving foolishly for anyone. Glancing in her rearview mirror, she saw the big car pulling into the oncoming lane to pass. Automatically, she slowed down as the other driver roared past. "Double idiot," she muttered.

She'd barely spoken when her engine started to sputter. Oh no! Kate knew she hadn't driven into any deep water. As her car rolled to a stop, she flattened her hands on the steering wheel in frustration. Then she noticed her gas gauge. Empty. Actually below empty. *Dumb bunny!* She plopped her head back.

At sixteen, when she'd gotten her first car, a VW

Bug, she'd run out of gas constantly, forgetting to check the gas or oil. One summer day on the way to the beach, she'd blown the engine because it didn't have a drop of oil in it. Since then, she'd made a concerted effort to monitor the fuel.

And now she was sitting in the rain with no gas and no one to call. Well, surely there had to be wreckers out here, she reasoned. Flipping open her phone, she paused. Number-one priority— don't worry her father. But she wasn't about to call Tucker for a second rescue. She tried information, got the number of a tow service and called. To her surprise, Owen Gibson answered. "Sheriff's office."

She pulled the phone away from her ear and stared at it. Surely she hadn't dialed that number.

"Sheriff's office," Owen repeated.

"Um... I'm sorry, I was trying to call a towing service," she explained.

"When Harold's not there, it goes to his cell. Then, if he's on a call, he forwards it here. I can page him, though."

Stumped, she didn't know what to say.

"Safety precaution," Owen explained. "You stranded somewhere?"

"Actually, yes. I feel really stupid. I ran out of gas."

"Where are you?"

She gave him the approximate coordinates and a description of her car. "Is there another garage that could just bring me some gas?"

"Someone'll be there," he promised.

Glancing at her phone, Kate wondered if she should call her father, explain why she was going to be late. As she tried to decide, she felt a gentle motion. Looking out to the side, she realized the car was slowly gliding downhill. She'd forgotten to change gears or put on the parking brake. Even though she knew it was going to kill her transmission, she ripped on the gear shift, putting the car in high gear and then setting the parking brake. Since the incline wasn't steep, the light car stopped.

Just as she sighed in relief, Kate saw the fast moving car that had passed her. It had fishtailed, was sliding off the road. Jumping out of her car, she was immediately drenched. The wind had increased, nearly knocking her back. Pushing wet hair out of her eyes, she saw the deep, wide patch of water she'd nearly driven into. It was hard to get a good view, but as she watched, to her horror, the other car kept sliding, going down the bank and plowing into the fast-filling gully.

At nearly the same time, she saw headlights approaching. Although her own were still on, Kate jumped up, waving her hands, hoping to stop the oncoming driver from slipping off the road.

The SUV stopped and Tucker stepped out, carrying a tire iron. Disregarding the water, he strode through the deep pool toward her.

She had to shout over the driving rain and wind as she pointed down the bank. "Car went down into the gully!"

"You all right?" Although the rain had drenched him to the point that she couldn't see his eyes, she could hear the concern his voice.

"Yes!"

"Call Owen, tell him what happened, then stay in your car."

Without waiting for a reply, Tucker climbed down the bank. Bare branches bent in the wind, flattening against the ground, but he still used them as handholds.

Rushing back to her car, Kate grabbed her phone and called Owen. As she clicked her phone off, she saw Alyssa get out of the SUV and wade toward the side of the road.

Galvanized, Kate leapt from her own car. "Alyssa! Stop!" The wind snatched away the words. Terrified for the girl's safety, Kate pushed her way through the water. The side of the road was no longer visible, and she didn't know if her next step would take her down into the gully. Worse, she was afraid Alyssa would fall.

Wading through the nearly waist-high water,

Kate tried to catch the girl. But the currents were fast, feeding down the bank. As she got close to Alyssa, Kate heard a popping explosion coming from below. Startled, she turned, seeing that Tucker had broken out the back windshield of the swamped car. The front end was completely immersed; the back was quickly sinking. Tucker pulled first a woman, then a man from the car. Snatches of the woman's screams pierced the noise of the storm.

Then Tucker turned back and climbed through the back window. Her heart nearly stopping, Kate stared in horror. As she did, Alyssa took another step and tumbled down the bank. Without thought, Kate plunged behind her, the water carrying her swiftly.

A strong swimmer, Kate dug in, hoping to out-distance Alyssa and catch her. Just then, Alyssa caught hold of a tree branch. Seeing that it was the branch of a still-rooted tree, Kate closed the distance and caught the branch, too. "Stay here," she shouted.

Although terrified, Alyssa shook her head. "Dad's gonna drown!"

"No!" Kate comforted Alyssa. "We won't let that happen!"

Releasing the branch, Kate fought her way to the car and grabbed the bumper. She gulped for breath. Tucker's head emerged through the windshield as he fought against the pull of the current. He kicked strongly, pushing himself out. With one arm he held on to a toddler.

He saw Kate and froze. Then he swam toward her. "I can't leave you out here!"

"Go!" she shouted back. "I'll hold onto the tree."

What color was left in his face drained when he spotted his daughter.

"Hang on!" Owen hollered from the bank.

Looking back, Kate saw a fire truck, tow truck, ambulance and a crowd of people gathering.

A rope landed in the water.

"Go!" Kate shouted.

Another rope landed close to Alyssa.

"Go!" Kate repeated.

As soon as he grabbed the rope, Kate released her grip on the bumper, fighting her way to Alyssa. Passing close to the rope, she grabbed it and held on until she could reach the tree.

Filled with fear, Alyssa held on until Kate reached her. With the current buffeting them, trying to suck them down the gully, it took precious minutes to get the rope around Alyssa. Before the girl could object, Kate let go so the rescuers could pull Alyssa to safety.

Exhausted, her chest heaving, Kate felt her fingers go numb as she clung to the branch. As she tried to put more pressure on it, the overstressed branch began to crack. But she didn't change her prayer: *Dear Lord, let Tucker and Alyssa be safe.*

Water from above and around her went down her throat. Her vision blurred, Kate couldn't tell if the entire tree she held on to was being uprooted.

Long, strong arms reached around her back, pulling and propping her up. Gasping, she recognized Tucker. Quickly, he put a rope around her waist, but didn't let go of her as he used his own anchor rope, held by men on the road, to pull them upward.

It seemed a dozen hands reached out to catch them when they got close enough to be pulled in. "Alyssa?" Kate gasped.

"Safe." Tucker held her close, not letting go. "You're both safe."

Volunteers crowded around them, helping Tucker and Kate reach Alyssa, who was with the paramedics. The nearly drowned couple and their child were in another ambulance not far away.

"Baby's going to be okay, Tucker!" Owen shouted. "You're a real hero."

Still shaking, Alyssa leapt up as soon as he stepped up into the second ambulance. "You're always my hero, Daddy," she cried, rainwater mixing with her tears.

Tucker engulfed Alyssa in a huge embrace, his voice cracking. "I told you to stay in the car." He smoothed back her dripping hair. "Oh, Lissy. What if I'd lost you?"

"That wouldn't happen." Still gulping out the words, Alyssa clung fiercely. "Mommy's watching out for us, just like she always said she would."

"Mommy *said* she'd watch over you?"

"Before she went to be with Jesus. Mommy knew it would be hardest on you, Daddy. But she said she'd always be with us."

Tucker's face crumpled as his chin hit his chest. He'd thought he was losing Lissy. And Kate... The image of losing Kate.... How had he not known that she had crept past every defense and lodged herself in his heart? He'd acknowledged that she had become his friend. But somehow, in the links of their friendship, he'd also invested his feelings. Feelings he never dreamed would again be rekindled. Somehow, they had slipped inside, wriggled past his wariness, breached his barriers.

Lifting his head, he looked at his daughter along with the woman he loved. And the heaviness he'd carried began to lift. He'd thought only of what the Lord had taken away, not of all he'd been given. Stretching out a grateful hand, he pulled Kate closer, never intending to let her go.

Chapter Eighteen

⟆

The next morning, legs tucked beneath her, Kate pulled the afghan up over her arms. Someone had uncovered her easel, revealing the new painting she'd been working on. She would have gotten up and put the cover back on if she had an ounce of energy. But Kate didn't want to leave the snug warmth of the chair.

"How about some more tea?" Daisy asked. "Or warm cocoa?"

Kate shook her head. "You've fussed over us till we're wearing you out."

Daisy had insisted that Tucker and Alyssa stay the night of the storm. After they'd changed into dry clothes the older woman had collected, she'd tucked them all in, then fed them some of her homemade chicken soup. When Kate hadn't returned on time, Marvin had called Daisy.

Unable to sit still, she'd prepared the soup while they waited for news.

An exhausted Alyssa quickly fell asleep in Kate's room. Kate crept in with her after a short time, worn out as well.

Tucker told them he had to get back and check on things, but Marvin reminded him that Owen was on duty, in charge until Tucker got some rest. Then Tucker insisted he could go home, but Daisy made a comfortable bed for him on the living room sofa. Once everyone was settled, Daisy took the overstuffed recliner in Kate's room for herself. Much like Dotey with her pups, Daisy didn't want anyone wandering out of her sight.

Daisy smiled, a fleeting touch of regret in her eyes. "I never had little ones of my own to fuss over."

Kate squeezed her hand. "Thank you, Daisy. I've loved the attention," she confessed. Looking up, she caught her father watching the interaction.

He rolled to her side. "In case you think I'm supposed to stop worrying just because you grew up…."

"I didn't stop worrying when you did," she teased back, wanting to erase his anxiety. "I truly did think to call, but everything happened so fast."

"As long as you're safe, Katie." He patted her arm. "Makes a person think about what's important, *really* important." Rolling toward the kitchen, he left her to think.

Tucker had left earlier, saying he needed to check in. Alyssa was content to stay and play with the puppies. Sipping her tea, Kate thought on the previous night and thanked the Lord for keeping them all safe.

"He's right," Tucker observed.

Startled, she nearly tipped the cup from its saucer. "I didn't know you were back."

"Rosewood's my responsibility. But so's my family."

"And she's safe."

He stepped closer.

Marvin suddenly whooped out in the kitchen. Kate and Tucker turned in the direction of the commotion. A grin nearly splitting his face, Marvin rolled into the room, Daisy by his side. "We're getting married!"

Shock, followed by teary happiness, hit Kate. "Oh, Dad." Jumping up, she let the afghan fall to the floor and ran to hug him. Then she hugged Daisy as well.

Alyssa had trailed them into the living room and hopped up to hug Marvin after Tucker shook his hand. In another, sweet but old-fashioned gesture, he lightly kissed Daisy's cheek.

Overcome by how much Tucker meant to her,

Kate felt the start of new tears. Not wanting to spoil her father's and Daisy's joy, she hid her face as she spoke. "We have some fresh-pressed apple juice in the kitchen we can use to celebrate. Remember, we got it at the kolache festival?"

Ducking into the kitchen, Kate caught her breath. She was thrilled for her father, but his news also meant he no longer needed her as his caregiver. One look at Daisy's face told Kate that her reasons for agreeing to marry Marvin had nothing to do with caregiving. Her eyes were filled with love.

And though Kate had treasured this time with her father, rebuilding their bond, becoming part of his church and community, Kate knew she was no longer needed.

Most importantly, Tucker had never voiced any feelings beyond friendship.

The phone rang. Absently, she picked up the receiver. It was the restoration manager from the Houston museum asking about her decision.

"I haven't really decided," Kate replied, fiddling with the tablecloth. "But I know you need an answer." Practically speaking, she could return to Houston as soon as her father married, which she explained. "I still need to find out some details." She tried to sound enthused. "It'll depend on when they set the wedding date. But…" The enthusiasm faded. "I don't suppose I have a good reason to stay here after that." Wiping away a tear, she put the receiver back.

"No reason to stay?" Tucker questioned quietly.

Kate whirled around.

"What about our family?"

She stared at him. "*Our* family?"

He took a step closer. "You know the one. Alyssa, Marvin, now Daisy. Oh, yeah. And me."

Kate wondered if she'd heard correctly.

He took another step, his boots thudding against the wood floor.

"Don't you know how much I love you, Kaitlyn Rose Lambert?"

Wanting to believe, her lips trembled. "How do you know you really can love again?"

"Faith." Tucker took her hand. "I've denied it, run away from it, railed at it. But the Lord didn't give up on me. And He kept you safe for me."

Kate swallowed the hot rush of emotion, her heart quaking.

In the quiet, she heard the mewling sounds of the puppies.

"It only took the pups a week to open their eyes." Tucker studied her intently. "Took me a lot longer. But I want what I see. And that's you."

Cautiously, she touched his jaw, her fingers tracing the strong line as she wondered if she was dreaming.

"You know the portrait you painted? The one I bought?" He reached up to clasp the hand that lingered by his face. 'There's only one thing missing in it. You."

She trembled beneath his touch. "I think there's room for me in the new one."

The sky, cleansed by the storm, was clear, allowing the light to pour in through the large window. Cupping her head with his other hand, he leaned so close that only the briefest breath separated them. His mouth against hers was both strong and gentle. Falling into his embrace, Kate closed her eyes, knowing he was hers to see forever.

Though Kate had never been married, she didn't feel the need for a big wedding. Especially after she and Tucker decided to buy a new home, one that would be a fresh start for both of them. New in a Rosewood sense. They'd chosen an old Victorian that had plenty of room for a studio, nursery, even Dotey and one of her pups. Her father and Daisy had adopted the other two.

Now, in the chapel with only their families and friends, she and Tucker were about to take the first step in that fresh start. Kate glanced down at Emma, grateful for her dear friend.

Even though the ceremony was small, Emma had insisted on designing the simple ivory dress

Kate requested. Kneeling, Emma fussed, making sure every silken fold was perfect.

Although Marvin was still in his wheelchair, he was going to give her away. Only fair turnaround, he'd teased, since Kate had given him away when he'd wed Daisy. Their nuptials had seemed so fast, but both insisted they didn't have the luxury of time.

Strains of organ music cascaded through the chapel and to the bride's room. Alyssa, already in place, winked at Kate, then started up the aisle, gently scattering rose petals.

Rising, Emma gave her a quick, light hug. "We can't wrinkle you. Oh, Kate, I know you'll be happy."

"Don't make me cry," Kate warned, feeling the tears lurking. "I look dreadful when my mascara's smeared."

"As matron-of-honor, I guess that *is* my duty." She brushed away a tear of her own. "Oh, dear."

Kate used her bouquet to gesture gently toward the aisle. "You're on."

Emma fell in line behind Alyssa.

Marvin rolled up. "I can remember when you used to play dress-up, and you always wanted to be the bride."

"Took me long enough for the real thing," she replied softly.

"Nope. Took you just the right time."

Together they traveled up the aisle. Daisy sat in the front pew, beaming. One of Tucker's oldest friends, Matt Whitaker, stood up for him as best man.

But it was Tucker Kate kept her gaze on. The love he proclaimed continued shining in his eyes, lighting her from within.

After passing her bouquet to Emma, Kate slipped her hand into Tucker's. It felt so right, as though they'd been forged to form a unique mold. He squeezed her fingers gently, keeping her close.

The age-old vows seemed to linger in the air, along with countless others that had been repeated where they stood. But theirs were special, Kate knew. As special as the bond they promised to keep, as special as the faith that now encircled them…as special as the love that made their hearts one.

* * * * *

Dear Reader,

We all have special memories that stay with us forever. My parents infused life with joy, hope and belief. And I have tried to infuse this story with those exceptional qualities.

Loss is as inevitable as life, but it's how we choose to treat the legacy that shapes our happiness. Tucker Grey has sustained a plentitude of loss, but he's blessed with a young daughter who needs him.

He also needs Kaitlyn Lambert's love so that together they can create not only a legacy but a family. An extended family that reaches out to all of us, the kind most of us either want or cherish.

In journeying again to Rosewood, I wish for you all to have the kindness, caring and love this special small town shares.

Blessings,

Bonnie K. Winn

QUESTIONS FOR DISCUSSION

1. Do you feel that Kate loses anything by leaving Houston for Rosewood?

2. Kate establishes a tight bond with Alyssa. Is this something you admire and/or understand?

3. Did you want to see Marvin remarry and have a new life with Daisy? Do you think love in our older years is as important as when we're young?

4. Could Tucker have taken some action to ease his mourning?

5. Have you ever felt let down by the Lord? If so, can you understand Tucker's perspective?

6. Rural life has been reshaped in America since the advent of superstores. Is it better or worse for the changes?

7. Would this story have worked if set in a large city? Why or why not?

8. Is the concept of neighbor helping neighbor timely or outdated? Are you friendly with your neighbors? Discuss.

9. Could you love someone else's child as your own? Did you believe Kate loved Alyssa in this way?

10. Kate initially chose the wrong man. Is it possible to choose the right one after such a mistake? Should she have trusted her instincts earlier?

11. Did you agree that Tucker's fellow church members should be so forgiving? Would you have judged his actions following his wife's death? Or treated him differently?

12. Kate decides to stay in Rosewood rather than go back to the big city. Do you agree with her choice? Would you have made a different choice? Discuss why or why not.

Here is an exciting sneak preview of
TWIN TARGETS by Marta Perry,
the first book in the new 6-book
Love Inspired Suspense series
PROTECTING THE WITNESSES
available beginning January 2010.

Deputy U.S. Marshal Micah McGraw forced down the sick feeling in his gut. A law enforcement professional couldn't get emotional about crime victims. He could imagine his police chief father saying the words. Or his FBI agent big brother. They wouldn't let emotion interfere with doing the job.

"Pity." The local police chief grunted.

Natural enough. The chief hadn't known Ruby Maxwell, aka Ruby Summers. He hadn't been the agent charged with relocating her to this supposedly safe environment in a small village in Montana. He didn't have to feel responsible for her death.

"This looks like a professional hit," Chief Burrows said.

"Yeah."

He knew only too well what was in the man's mind. What would a professional hit man be doing in the remote reaches of western Montana?

Why would anyone want to kill this seemingly inoffensive waitress?

And most of all, what did the U.S. Marshals Service have to do with it?

All good questions. Unfortunately he couldn't answer any of them. Secrecy was the crucial element that made the Federal Witness Protection Service so successful. Breach that, and everything that had been gained in the battle against organized crime would be lost.

His cell buzzed and he turned away to answer it. "McGraw."

"You wanted the address for the woman's next of kin?" asked one of his investigators.

"Right." Ruby had a twin sister, he knew. She'd have to be notified. Since she lived back east, at least he wouldn't be the one to do that.

"Jade Summers. Librarian. Current address is 45 Rock Lane, White Rock, Montana."

For an instant Micah froze. "Are you sure of that?"

"'Course I'm sure."

After he hung up, Micah turned to stare once more at the empty shell that had been Ruby Summers. She'd made mistakes in her life, plenty of them, but she'd done the right thing in the end when she'd testified against the mob. She hadn't deserved to end up lifeless on a cold concrete floor.

As for her sister…

What exactly was an easterner like Jade Summers doing in a small town in Montana? If there was an innocent reason, he couldn't think of it.

Ruby must have tipped her off to her location. That was the only explanation, and the deed violated one of the major principles of witness protection.

Ruby had known the rules. Immediate family could be relocated with her. If they chose not to, no contact was permitted—ever.

Ruby's twin had moved to Montana. White Rock was probably forty miles or so east of Billings. Not exactly around the corner from her sister.

But the fact that she was in Montana had to mean that they'd been in contact. And that contact just might have led to Ruby's death.

He glanced at his watch. Once his team arrived, he'd get back on the road toward Billings and beyond, to White Rock. To find Jade Summers and get some answers.

* * * * *

Will Micah get to Jade in time to
save her from a similar fate?
Find out in TWIN TARGETS,
available January 2010
from Love Inspired Suspense.

Love Inspired®
SUSPENSE
RIVETING INSPIRATIONAL ROMANCE

These contemporary tales
of intrigue and romance
feature Christian characters
facing challenges to their faith...
and their lives!

**Four new Love Inspired Suspense titles are
available every month wherever books are
sold, including most bookstores, supermarkets,
drug stores and discount stores.**

Steeple
Hill®

Visit:
www.steeplehillbooks.com